THE WORKS OF ANATOLE FRANCE
IN AN ENGLISH TRANSLATION
EDITED BY FREDERIC CHAPMAN

THE WHITE STONE

THE WHITE STONE

BY ANATOLE FRANCE

 ### A TRANSLATION BY
CHARLES E. ROCHE

LONDON: JOHN LANE, THE BODLEY HEAD
NEW YORK: DODD, MEAD AND COMPANY
MCMXXV

Published in U. S. A., 1922
by
DODD, MEAD AND COMPANY, INC.

PRINTED IN U. S. A.

VAIL-BALLOU COMPANY
BINGHAMTON AND NEW YORK

Καὶ ἐμοιγε δοκειτε ἐπὶ λευκαδα πέτρην καὶ δῆμον ὀνείρωων
καταδαρθεντες τοσαῦτα ὀνειροπολεῖν ἐν ἀκαρεῖ τῆς νυκτός οὔσης·
(Philopatris, xxi.)

And to me it seems that you have fallen asleep
upon a white rock, and in a parish of dreams, and
have dreamt all this in a moment while it was
night.

CONTENTS

THE WHITE STONE

I

 FEW Frenchmen, united in friendship, who were spending the spring in Rome, were wont to meet amid the ruins of the disinterred Forum. They were Joséphin Leclere, an Embassy Attaché on leave; M. Goubin, licencié ès lettres, an annotator; Nicole Langelier, of the old Parisian family of the Langeliers, printers and classical scholars; Jean Boilly, a civil engineer, and Hippolyte Dufresne, a man of leisure, and a lover of the fine arts.

Towards five o'clock of the afternoon of the first day of May, they wended their way, as was their custom, through the northern door, closed to the public, where Commendatore Boni, who superintended the excavations, welcomed them with quiet amenity, and led them to the threshold of his house of wood nestling in the shadow of laurel bushes, privet hedges and cytisus, and rising above the vast trench, dug down to the depth of the ancient Forum, in the cattle market of pontifical Rome.

Here, they pause awhile, and look about them.

Facing them rise the truncated shafts of the
Columnæ Honorariæ, and where stood the Basilica
of Julia, the eye rested on what bore the semblance
of a huge draughts-board and its draughts.
Further south, the three columns of the Temple of
the Dioscuri cleave the azure of the skies with their
blue-tinted volutes. On their right, surmounting
the dilapidated Arch of Septimus Severus, the tall
columns of the Temple of Saturn, the dwellings of
Christian Rome, and the Women's Hospital display
in tiers, their facings yellower and muddier than the
waters of the Tiber. To their left stands the Palatine flanked by huge red arches and crowned with
evergreen oaks. At their feet, from hill to hill,
among the flagstones of the Via Sacra, narrow as a
village street, spring from the earth an agglomeration of brick walls and marble foundations, the
remains of buildings which dotted the Forum in the
days of Rome's strength. Trefoil, oats, and the
grasses of the field which the wind has sown on their
lowered tops, have covered them with a rustic roof
illumined by the crimson poppies. A mass of
débris, of crumbling entablatures, a multitude of
pillars and altars, an entanglement of steps and
enclosing walls: all this indeed not stunted but of
a serried vastness and within limits.

Nicole Langelier was doubtless reviewing in his
mind the host of monuments confined in this famed
space:

"These edifices of wise proportions and moderate dimensions," he remarked, "were separated from one another by narrow streets full of shade. Here ran the *vicoli* beloved in countries where the sun shines, while the generous descendants of Remus, on their return from hearing public speakers, found, along the walls of the temples, cool yet foul-smelling corners, whence the rinds of water-melons and castaway shells were never swept away, and where they could eat and enjoy their siesta. The shops skirting the square must certainly have emitted the pungent odour of onions, wine, fried meats, and cheese. The butchers' stalls were laden with meats, to the delectation of the hardy citizens, and it was from one of those butchers that Virginius snatched the knife with which he killed his daughter. There also were doubtless jewellers and vendors of little domestic tutelary deities, protectors of the hearth, the ox-stall, and the garden. The citizens' necessaries of life were all centred in this spot. The market and the shops, the basilicas, *i. e.,* the commercial Exchanges and the civil tribunals; the Curia, that municipal council which became the administrative power of the universe; the prisons, whose vaults emitted their much dreaded and fetid effluvia, and the temples, the altars, of the highest necessity to the Italians who have ever some thing to beg of the celestial powers.

"Here it was, lastly, that during a long roll of

centuries were accomplished the vulgar or strange deeds, almost ever flat and dull, oftentimes odious and ridiculous, at times generous, the agglomeration of which constitutes the august life of a people."

"What is it that one sees, in the centre of the square, fronting the commemorative pedestals?" inquired M. Goubin, who, primed with an eye-glass, had noticed a new feature in the ancient Forum, and was thirsting for information concerning it.

Joséphin Leclerc obligingly answered him that they were the foundations of the recently unearthed colossal statue of Domitian.

Thereupon he pointed out, one after the other, the monuments laid bare by Giacomo Boni in the course of his five years' fruitful excavations: the fountain and the well of Juturna, under the Palatine Hill; the altar erected on the site of Cæsar's funeral pile, the base of which spread itself at their feet, opposite the Rostra; the archaic stele and the legendary tomb of Romulus over which lies the black marble slab of the Comitium; and again, the Lacus Curtius.

The sun, which had set behind the Capitol, was striking with its last shafts the triumphal arch of Titus on the towering Velia. The heavens, where to the West the pearl-white moon floated, remained as blue as at midday. An even, peaceful, and clear shadow spread itself over the silent Forum. The bronzed navvies were delving this field of stones, while, pursuing the work of the ancient Kings, their comrades turned the crank of a well, for the purpose of drawing the water which still forms the bed where slumbered, in the days of pious Numa, the reed-fringed Velabrum.

They were performing their task methodically and with vigilance. Hippolyte Dufresne, who had for several months been a witness of their assiduous labour, of their intelligence and of their prompt obedience to orders, inquired of the director of the excavations how it was that he obtained such yeoman's work from his labourers.

"By leading their life," replied Giacomo Boni. "Together with them do I turn over the soil; I impart to them what we are together seeking for, and I impress on their minds the beauty of our common work. They feel an interest in an enterprise the grandeur of which they apprehend but vaguely. I have seen their faces pale with enthusiasm when unearthing the tomb of Romulus. I am their everyday comrade, and if one of them falls ill, I take a seat at his bedside. I place as great faith in them as they do in me. And so it is that I boast of faithful workmen."

"Boni, my dear Boni," exclaimed Joséphin Leclerc, "you know full well that I admire your labours, and that your grand discoveries fill me with emotion, and yet, allow me to say so, I regret the days when flocks grazed over the entombed Forum. A white ox, from whose massive head branched horns widely apart, chewed the cud in the unploughed field; a hind dozed at the foot of a tall column which sprang from the sward, and one mused: Here was debated the fate of the world. The Forum has been lost to poets and lovers from the day that it ceased to be the Campo Formio."

Jean Boilly dwelt on the value of these excavations, so methodically carried out, as a contribution towards a knowledge of the past. Then, the conversation having drifted towards the philosophy of the history of Rome:

"The Latins," he remarked, "displayed reason even in the matter of their religion. Their gods were commonplace and vulgar, but full of common sense and occasionally generous. If a comparison be drawn between this Roman Pantheon composed of soldiers, magistrates, virgins, and matrons and the deviltries painted on the walls of Etruscan tombs, reason and madness will be found in juxtaposition. The infernal scenes depicted in the mortuary chambers of Corneto represent the monstrous creations of ignorance and fear. They seem to us as grotesque as Orcagna's *Day of Judgment* in Santa Maria Novella at Florence, and the *Dantesque Hell* of the Campo Santo of Pisa, whereas the Latin Pantheon reflects for ever the image of a well-organised society. The gods of the Romans were like themselves, industrious and good citizens. They were useful deities, each one having its proper function. The very nymphs held civil and political offices.

"Look at Juturna, whose altar at the foot of the Palatine we have so frequently contemplated. She did not seem fated by her birth, her adventures, and her misfortunes to occupy a permanent post in the city of Romulus. An incensed Rutula, beloved by Jupiter, who rewarded her with immortality, when King Turnus fell by the hand of Æneas, as decreed by the Fates, she flung herself into the Tiber, to escape thus from the light of day, since it was denied her to perish with her royal brother. Long did the shepherds of Latium tell the story of the living nymph's lamentations from the depths of the river. In later years, the villagers of rural Rome, when looking down at night-time over the bank, imagined that they could see her by the moon's rays, lurking in her glaucous garments among the rushes. The Romans, however, did not leave her to the idle contemplation of her sorrows. They promptly conceived the idea of allotting to her an important duty, and entrusted her with the custody of their fountains, converting her into a municipal goddess. And so it is with all their divinities. The Dioscuri, whose temple lives in its beautiful ruins, the Dioscuri, the brothers of Helen, the sparkling *Gemini*, were put to good use by the Romans, as messengers of the State. The Dioscuri it was, who, mounted on a white charger, brought to Rome the news of the victory of Lake Regillus.

"The Italians asked of their gods only temporal and substantial benefits. In this respect, notwithstanding the Asiatic fears which have invaded Europe, their religious sentiment has not changed. That which they formally demanded from their gods and their genii, they nowadays expect from the Madonna and the Saints. Every parish possesses its Beatified patron, to whom requests are preferred just as in the case of a Deputy. There are Saints for the vine, for cereals, for cattle, for the colic, and for toothache. Latin imagination has repeopled Heaven with a multitude of living bodies, and has converted Judaic monotheism into a new polytheism. It has enlivened the Gospels with a copious mythology; it has re-established a familiar intercourse between the divine and the terrestrial world. The peasantry demand miracles of their protecting Saints, and hurl invectives at them if the miracle is slow of manifestation. The peasant who has in vain solicited a favour of the Bambino, returns to the chapel, and addressing on this occasion the Incoronata herself, exclaims:

" 'I am not speaking to you, you whoreson, but to your sainted mother.'

"The women make the Madre di Dio a confidant of their love affairs. They believe with some show of reason that being a woman she understands, and that there is no need to be on a footing of delicacy with her. They have no fear of going too far—a proof of their piety. Hence we must view with admiration the prayer which a fine lass of the Genoese Riviera addressed to the Madonna: 'Holy Mother of God, who didst conceive without sin, grant me the grace of sinning without conceiving.' "

Nicole Langelier here remarked that the religion of the Romans lent itself to the evolution of Rome's policy.

"Bearing the stamp of a distinctly national character," he said, "it was, for all that, capable of penetrating the minds of foreign nations, and of winning them over by its sociable and tolerant spirit. It was an administrative religion propagating itself without effort together with the rest of the administration."

"The Romans loved war," said M. Goubin, who studiously avoided paradoxes.

"They loved not war for itself," was Jean Boilly's rejoinder. "They were far too reasonable for that. That military service was to them a hardship is revealed by certain signs. Monsieur Michel Bréal tells you that the word which primarily expressed the equipment of the soldier, *ærumna*, subsequently assumed the general meaning of lassitude, need, trouble, hardship, toil, pain, and distress. Those peasants were just as other peasants.

They entered the ranks merely because compelled and forced thereto. Their very leaders, the wealthy proprietors, waged war neither for pleasure nor for glory. Previous to entering on a campaign, they consulted their interests twenty times over, and carefully computed the chances."

"True," said M. Goubin, "but their circumstances and the state of the world compelled them ever to be in arms. Thus it is that they carried civilisation to the far ends of the known world. War is above all an instrument of progress."

"The Latins," resumed Jean Boilly, "were agriculturists who waged agriculturists' wars. Their ambitions were ever agricultural. They exacted of the vanquished, not money, but soil, the whole or part of the territory of the subjugated confederation, generally speaking one-third, out of friendship, as they said, and because they were moderate in their desires. The farmer came and drove his plough over the spot where the legionary had a short while ago planted his pike. The tiller of the soil confirmed the soldier's conquests. Admirable soldiers, doubtless, well disciplined, patient, and brave, who fought and who were sometimes beaten just like any others; yet still more admirable peasants. If wonder is felt at their having conquered so many lands, still more is it to be wondered at that they should have kept them. The marvel of it is that in spite of the many battles they lost, these stubborn peasants never yielded an acre of soil, so to speak."

While this discussion was proceeding, Giacomo Boni was gazing with a hostile eye at the tall brick house standing to the north of the Forum on top of several layers of ancient substructures.

"We are about," he said, "to explore the Curia Julia. We shall soon, I hope, be in a position to break up the sordid building which covers its remains. It will not cost the State much to purchase it for the spade's work. Buried under nine mètres of soil on which stands the Convent of S. Adriano lie the flagstones of Diocletian, who restored the Curia for the last time. We shall surely find among the rubbish a number of the marble tables on which the laws were engraved. It is a matter of interest to Rome, to Italy, nay to the whole world, that the last vestiges of the Roman Senate should see the light of day."

Thereupon he invited his friends into his hut, as hospitable and rustic a one as that of Evander.

It constituted a single room wherein stood a deal table laden with black potteries and shapeless fragments giving out an earthy smell.

"Prehistorical treasures!" sighed Joséphin Leclerc. "And so, my good Giacomo Boni, not content with seeking in the Forum the monuments of the Emperors, those of the Republic, and those of the Kings, you must fain sink down into the soil which bore flora and fauna that have vanished, drive your spade into the quaternary, and the tertiary, penetrate the pliocene, the miocene, and the eocene; from Latin archæology you wander to prehistoric archæology and to palæontology. The salons are expressing alarm at the depths to which you are venturing. Countess Pasolini would like to know where you intend to stop, and you are represented in a little satirical sheet as coming out at the Antipodes, breathing the words: *Adesso va bene!*"

Boni seemed not to have heard.

He was examining with deep attention a clay vessel still damp and covered with ooze. His pale blue expressive eyes darkened while critically examining this humble work of man for some unrevealed trace of a mysterious past, but resumed their natural hue as the Commendatore's mind wandered off into a reverie.

"These remains which you have before you," he presently remarked, "these roughly hewn little wooden sarcophagi and these cinerary urns of black pottery and of house-like shape containing calcined bones were gathered under the Temple of Faustina, on the north-west side of the Forum.

"Black urns containing ashes, and skeletons resting in their coffins as if in a bed, are here to be met with side by side. The funeral rites of the Greeks and the Romans included both those of burial and

of cremation. Over the whole of Europe, in prehistoric days, the two customs were simultaneously
observed, in the same city and in the same tribe.
Does this dual fashion of sepulture correspond with
the ideals of two races? I am inclined to believe
so."

Picking up with reverential and almost ritual
gesture, an urn shaped like a dwelling and containing a small quantity of ashes, he went on:

"The men who in immemorial times gave this
form to clay, believed that the soul, being attached
to the bones and the ashes, had need of a dwelling,
but that it did not require a very large house
wherein to live the abridged life of the dead.
These men were of a noble race which came from
Asia. The one whose light ashes I now hold lived
before the days of Evander and of the shepherd
Faustulus."

Then, making use of the phraseology of the
ancients, he added:

"Those were the days when King Vitulus, King
Calf as we should say, held peaceful sway over this
country so pregnant with glory. Monotonous
pastoral times reigned over the Ausonian plain.
These men were, however, neither ignorant nor
boorish. Much priceless knowledge had come to
them from their forefathers. Both the ship and
the oar were known to them. They practised the
art of subjecting oxen to the yoke and of harnessing

them to the pole. They kindled at will the divine flame. They gathered salt, wrought in gold, kneaded and baked vases of clay. Probably too they began to till the soil. They do say that the Latin shepherds became agricultural labourers in the fabled days of the Calf. They cultivated millet, wheat, and spelt. They stitched skins together with needles of bone. They wove and perchance made wool false to its whiteness by dyeing it various colours. By the phases of the moon did they measure time. They gazed upon the heavens but to discover in them what was in the world below. They saw in them the greyhound who watches for Diospiter the shepherd who tends the starry flock. The prolific clouds were to them the Sun's cattle, the cows supplying milk to the cerulean countryside. They worshipped the heavens as their Father, and the Earth as their Mother. At eventide, they heard the chariots of the gods, like themselves migratory, roll along the mountain roads with their ponderous wheels. They enjoyed the light of day and pondered with sadness over the life of the souls in the Kingdom of Shadows.

"We know that these massive-headed Aryans were fair, since their gods, made to their own image, were fair. Indra had locks like ears of wheat and a beard as tawny as the tiger's coat. The Greeks conceived the immortal gods with blue or glaucous eyes, and a head of golden hair. The goddess Roma was *flava et candida:*

"Were it possible to make a whole out of these calcined bony fragments, the result would be pure Aryan forms. In those massive and vigorous skulls, in those heads as square as the primary Rome which their sons were to build, you would recognise the ancestors of the patricians of the Commonwealth, the long flourishing stock which produced tribunes of the people, pontiffs, and consuls; you would be handling the magnificent mould of the robust brains which constructed religion, the family, the army, and the public laws of the most strongly organised city that ever existed."

Gently placing the bit of pottery on the rustic table, Giacomo Boni bends over a coffin the size of a cradle, a coffin dug out of the trunk of an oak, and similar in shape to the early canoes of man. He lifts up the thin covering of bark and sap-wood forming the lid of that funeral wherry, and brings to light bones as frail as a bird's skeleton. Of the body, there hardly remains the spinal column, and it would bear resemblance to one of the lowest of vertebrata, such as a big saurian, did not the fulness of the forehead reveal man. Coloured beads, which have become detached from a necklace, are scattered over these bones browned with age, washed by subterranean waters, and exhumed from clayey soil.

"Look!" says Boni, "at this little boy who was not given the honours of cremation, but buried, and returned as a whole to the earth whence he sprung. He is not a son of headmen, nor a noble inheritor of the traits of a fair race. He belongs to the race indigenous to the Mediterranean, the race which became the Roman *plebs*, and which supplies Italy to the present day with subtle lawyers and calculating individuals. He was born in the Palatine City of the Seven Hills, in days seen dimly through the mist of heroic fables. It is a Romulean boy. In those days, the Valley of the Seven Hills was a morass, and the slopes of the Palatine were covered with reed-thatched huts only. A tiny lance was placed on the coffin to show that the child was a male. He was barely four years old when he fell asleep in death. Then his mother clothed him with a beautiful tunic clasped at the neck, around which she fastened a string of beads. The kinsmen did not begrudge him their offerings. They deposited on his tomb, in urns of black earthenware, milk, beans, and a bunch of grapes. I have collected these vessels and I have fashioned similar ones out of the same clay by the heat of a wood fire lit in the Forum at night. Previous to taking a last farewell of him, they ate and drank together a portion of their offerings; this funeral repast assuaged their sorrow. Child, thou who sleepest since the days of the god Quirinus, an Empire has passed over thy agrestic coffin, and the same stars which shone at thy birth are about to light up the skies above us. The unfathomable space which separates the hours of your life from those of our own constitutes but an imperceptible moment in the life of the Universe."

After a moment's silence, Nicole Langelier remarked:

"It is as difficult to distinguish amid a people the races composing it as to trace in the course of a river the streams which mingle with it. What constitutes, moreover, a race? Do any human races really exist? I see white men, red men, and black men. But, they do not constitute races; they are merely varieties of the same race, of the same species, which form together fruitful unions and intermingle without ceasing. *A fortiori*, the man of learning knows not several yellow races or several white races. Human beings invent, however, races in pursuance of their vanity, their hatred, or their greed. In 1871, France became dismembered by virtue of the rights of the Germanic race, and yet no German race has an existence. The antisemites kindle the hatred of Christian peoples against the Jews, and still there is no Jewish race.

"What I state on the subject, Boni, is purely speculative, and not with the view of running counter to your ideas. How could one not believe you! Conviction has its home on your lips. Moreover, you blend in your thoughts the profound verities of poetry with the far-spreading truths of science. As you truly state, the shepherds who came from Bactriana peopled Greece and Italy. As you again say, they found there natives of the soil. In ancient days, a belief shared in common by Italians and Hellenes was that the first men who peopled their country were like Erectheus, born of Mother Earth. Nor do I pretend, my dear Boni, that you cannot trace through the centuries the autochthones of your Ausonia, and the immigrants from the Pamir; the former, intelligent and eloquent plebeians; the latter, patricians fully impregnated with courage and faith. For, when all is said, if there are not, properly speaking, several human races, and if still less so several white races, our species assuredly comprises distinct varieties oftentimes stamped with marked characteristics. Hence there is nothing to hinder two or more of these varieties living for a long time side by side without fusing, each one preserving its individual characteristics. Nay, these differences may occasionally, in lieu of vanishing with the course of time under the action of the plastic forces of nature, on the contrary become accentuated more strongly through the empire of immutable customs, and the stress of social institutions."

"*E proprio vero,*" said Boni in a low tone, as he

replaced the oaken lid on the coffin of the Romulean child.

Then, begging his guests to be seated, he said to Nicole Langelier:

"I shall now hold you to your promise, and beg you to read to us that story of Gallio, at which I have seen you at work in your little room in the *Foro Traiano.* You make Romans speak in your script. This is the spot to hear your narrative, here in a corner of the Forum, close by the Via Sacra, between the Capitol and the Palatine. Tarry not with your reading, so as not to be over-taken by the twilight, and lest your voice be quickly drowned by the cries of the birds warning one another of approaching night."

The guests of Giacomo Boni welcomed the fore-going utterance with a murmur of approval, and Nicole Langelier, without waiting for more pressing entreaties, unrolled a manuscript and read aloud the following narrative.

II

GALLIO

N the 804th year of the foundation of Rome, and the 13th of the principality of Claudius Cæsar, Junius Annæus Novatus was pro-consul of Achaia. Born of a knightly family of Spanish origin, a son of Seneca the Rhetor and of the chaste Helvia, a brother of Annæus Mela, and of the famed Lucius Annæus, he bore the name of his adopted father, the Rhetor Gallio, exiled by Tiberius. In his mother's veins flowed the same blood as that of Cicero, and he had inherited from his father, together with immense wealth, a love of letters and of philosophy. He studied the works of the Greeks even more assiduously than those of the Latins. His mind was a prey to noble aspiration. He was an interested student of nature and of what appertains to her. The activity of his intelligence was so keen that he enjoyed being read to while in his bath, and that, even when joining in the chase, he was wont to carry with him his tablets of wax and his stylus. During the leisure moments which he managed to secure in the intervals of most serious duties and most

important works, he wrote books on subjects relating to nature, and composed tragedies.

His clients and his freedmen loudly proclaimed his gentleness. His was indeed a genial character. He had never been known to give way to a fit of anger. He looked upon violence as the worst and most unpardonable of weaknesses.

All deeds of cruelty were held in execration by him, save when their true character escaped him owning to the consecration of custom and of public opinion. He frequently discovered, amid the severities rendered sacred by ancestral usage and sanctified by the laws, revolting excesses against which he raised his voice in protest, and which he would have attempted to sweep away, had not the interests of the State and the common welfare been objected from all quarters. In those days, conscientious magistrates and honest functionaries were not few and far between throughout the Empire. There were indeed a number as honest and as impartial as Gallio himself, but it is to be doubted whether another could be found so humane.

Entrusted with the administration of that Greece despoiled of her riches, her pristine glory departed, and fallen from her freedom so full of life into an idle tranquillity, he remembered that she had formerly taught the world wisdom and the fine arts, and his treatment of her combined the vigilance of a guardian with the reverence of a son. He

respected the liberties of the cities and the rights
of individuals. He showed honour to those who
were truly Greeks by birth and education regretting
that their numbers were sorely restricted, and that
his authority extended for the greater part over an
infamous rabble of Jews and Syrians; yet he
remained equitable in dealing with these Asiatics,
laying unction to his soul for what he considered a
meritorious endeavour.

He dwelt in Corinth, the richest and most densly
populated city of Roman Greece. His villa, built
in the time of Augustus, enlarged and embellished
since then by the pro-consuls who had governed the
province in succession, stood on the furthermost
western slopes of the Acrocorinthus, whose foliaged
summit was crowned by the Temple of Venus and
the groves where dwelt her priests. It was a somewhat spacious mansion surrounded by gardens
studded with bushy trees, watered by springs, ornamented with statues, alcoves, gymnasia, baths, libraries, and altars consecrated to the gods.

He was strolling in it on a certain morn, according to his wont, with his brother Annæus Mela,
discoursing on the order of nature and the vicissi-
tudes of fortune. The sun was rising, hazy in its
white splendour in the roseate heavens. The
gentle undulations of the hills of the Isthmus concealed the Saronic shore, the Stadium, the sanctuary
of the sports, and the eastern harbour of Cenchreæ.

Between the fallow slopes of the Geranean range and the crimson twin-peaked Helicon, one could, however, obtain a glimpse of the quiescent blue waters of the Alcyonium Mare. In the distance, and to the north, glistened the three snow-capped summits of Parnassus. Gallio and Mela proceeded together as far as the edge of the elevated foreground. At their feet spread Corinth standing on an extensive plateau of pale yellow sand, and sloping gently towards the spumous fringe of the Gulf. The pavements of the forum, the columns of the basilica, the tiers of the hippodrome, the white steps of the porches sparkled, while the gilded roofs of the temples flashed dazzling rays. Vast and new, the town was intersected with straight-running streets. A wide road descended to the harbour of Lechæum, whose shore was fringed with warehouses and whose waters were covered with ships. To the west, the atmosphere reeked with the smoke of the iron-foundries, while the streams ran black from the pollution of the dye-houses, and on that side, forests of pine extending to the edge of the horizon, were lost to sight in the skies.

Gradually, the town awoke from its slumbers. The strident neighing of a horse rent the morning calm, and soon were heard the muffled rumblings of wheels, shouting of waggoners, and the chanting voices of women selling herbs. Emerging from their hovels amid the ruins of the Palace of

Sisyphus, aged and blind hags bearing copper vessels on their heads, and led by children, wended their way to draw water from the Pirene fountain. On the flat roofs of the houses abutting the grounds of the proconsul, Corinthian women were spreading linen to dry, and one of them was castigating her child with leek-stalks. In the hollow road leading to the Acropolis, a semi-nude old bronze-coloured man, prodded the rump of an ass laden with salad herbs and chanted between the stumps of his teeth and in his unkempt beard, a slave-song:

> "Toil, little ass,
> As I have toiled.
> Much good will it do you:
> You may be sure of it."

Meanwhile, at the sight of the town resuming its daily labour, Gallio fell a-musing over the earlier Corinth, the lovely Ionian city, opulent and joyous until the day when she witnessed the massacre of her citizens by the soldiery of Mummius, her women, the noble daughters of Sisyphus, sold at auction, her palaces and temples the prey of flames, her walls razed to the ground, and her riches piled away into the Liburnian ships of the Consul.

"Hardly a century ago," he remarked, "the work wrought by Mummius still stood revealed in all its horror. The shore which you see, brother mine, was more of a desert than the Libyan sands. The divine Julius rebuilt the town wrecked by our arms, and peopled it with freedmen. On this very strand, where the illustrious Bacchiadæ formerly revelled in their haughty indolence, poor and rude Latins settled, and Corinth entered upon a new lease of life. She grew rapidly, and realised how to take advantage of her position. She levies tribute on all ships which, whether from the East or from the West, cast anchor in her two harbours of Lechæum and Cenchreæ. Her population and wealth increase apace under the ægis of the Roman peace.

"What blessings has not the Empire bestowed throughout the world! To the Empire is due the profound tranquillity which the countryside enjoys. The seas are swept of pirates, and the highways of robbers. From the befogged Ocean to the Permulic Gulf, from Gades to the Euphrates, the trading of merchandise proceeds in undisturbed security. The law protects the lives and property of all. Individual rights must not be infringed upon. Liberty has henceforth no other limits than its lines of defence, and is circumscribed for its own security alone. Justice and reason rule the world."

Unlike his two brothers, Annæus Mela had not intrigued for honours. Those who loved him, and their name was legion, for he was ever in his intercourse affable and extremely pleasant, attributed his detachment from public affairs to the moderation of a mind attracted by the blessings of tranquil obscurity, a mind which had no other care than the study of philosophy. But those who observed him with greater insight were under the impression that he was ambitious after his own fashion, and that like Mæcenas, he, a simple knight, was consumed with the envy of enjoying the same consideration as the consuls. Lastly, certain evil-minded individuals believed that they discerned in him the greed of the Senecas for the riches which they affected to despise, and thus did they explain to themselves that Mela had for a long time lived in obscurity in Betica, giving himself up entirely to the management of his vast estates, and that subsequently summoned to Rome by his brother the philosopher, he had devoted himself to the administration of the finances of the Empire, rather than go in the quest of high judiciary or military posts. His character could not be readily determined from his utterances, for he spoke the language of the Stoics, a language equally adapted for the concealment of the weaknesses of the mind and the revelation of the grandeur of one's sentiments. It was in those days the height of elegance to utter virtuous discourse. At any rate, there is no doubt that Mela spoke his thoughts.

He replied to his brother that, although not versed in public affairs like himself, he had had occasion to admire the power and wisdom of the Romans.

"They reveal themselves," he said, "in the most remote parts of our own Spain.   But it is in a wild pass of the mountains of Thessaly that I have been made to appreciate at its highest the beneficent majesty of the Empire.   I had come from Hypata, a town renowned for its cheeses, and whose women were notorious for witchcraft, and I had been riding for some hours along mountain paths, without coming across a human face.   Overcome by the heat and fatigue, I tethered my horse to a tree by the road, and lay down under an arbutus-bush.   I had been resting there a short while only, when there came along a lean old man bowed down under a load of branches.   Utterly exhausted, he tottered in his steps, and just as he was about to fall exclaimed: 'Cæsar.'   On hearing such an invocation escape the lips of a poor woodcutter in this stony solitude, my heart overflowed with veneration for the tutelary City, which inspires, even unto the farthermost lands, the most rustic of minds with so great a conception of its sovereign providence. But sadness and a feeling of distress mingled with my admiration, brother mine, when I reflected upon the injury and insults to which the inheritance of Augustus and the fortune of Rome were exposed through men's folly and the vices of the century."

"I have witnessed on the spot, brother mine," replied Gallio, "the crimes and follies which sadden your mind.   My cheek has blanched under the gaze of the victims of Caius from my seat in the Senate. I have held my peace, as I did not despair of better days. I am of the opinion that good citizens should serve the Republic under bad princes rather than shirk their duty in a useless death."

As Gallio was uttering these sentiments, two men, still in their youth and wearing the toga, came up to him. The one was Lucius Cassius, of a Roman family, plebeian but ancient, and having attained distinction. The other, Marcus Lollius, son and grandson of consuls, and moreover of a knightly family, which had sprung from the free town of Terracina. Both had frequented the schools of Athens, and acquired a knowledge of the laws of nature of which those Romans who had not been in Greece were totally ignorant.

At the present moment, they were studying in Corinth the management of public affairs, and the proconsul surrounded himself with them as an ornamental adjunct to his magistracy. Somewhat behind them, the Greek Apollodorus, wearing the short cape of the philosophers, bald of head, and with Socratic beard, sauntered along, with uplifted arm and gesticulating fingers, discussing with himself.

Gallio welcomed all three of them in kindly fashion.

"The rose of dawn is already fading," he said, "and the sun is beginning to shed its steeled darts.

Come along, my good friends, to the coolness of the shady foliage beyond."

Saying this, he led them along the banks of a stream whose babbling murmur invited peaceful reflections, until they had reached an enclosure of verdant bushes in the midst of which lay in a hollow an alabaster basin filled with limpid waters on whose surface floated the feather of a dove, which had just bathed in them, and which was now cooing plaintively from a branch. They took their seats on a semicircular marble bench supported by griffins. Laurel and myrtle bushes blended their shadows about it. Statues encircled the enclosure. A wounded Amazon gracefully coiled her arm about her head. Grief appeared a thing of beauty on her lovely face. A shaggy Satyr was playing with a goat. A Venus, emerging from the bath, was drying her wetted limbs along which a shudder of pleasurable emotion seemed to run. Near by, a youthful Faun was smilingly placing a flute to his lips. His face was partly concealed by the branches, but his shining belly glistened amid the leafage.

"That Faun seems animated," remarked Marcus Lollius. "One could imagine that a gentle breathing was causing his bosom to heave."

"He is true to life, Marcus," said Gallio. "One expects to hear rustic melodies flow from his flute. A Greek slave carved him out of the marble, in imitation of an ancient model. The Greeks formerly excelled in the making of these fanciful statues. Several of their efforts in this style are justly renowned. There is no gainsaying it: they have found the means of giving august traits to the gods and of expressing in both marble and bronze the majesty of the masters of the world. Who but admires the Olympian Zeus? And yet, who would care to be Phidias!"

"No Roman would assuredly care to be Phidias," exclaimed Lollius, who was spending the fortune he had inherited from his ancestry in ornamenting his villa at Pausilypum with the masterpieces of Phidias and Myron brought over from Greece and Asia.

Lucius Cassius was of the same opinion. He argued with some warmth that the hands of a free man were not made to wield the sculptor's chisel or the painter's brush, and that no Roman citizen would condescend to the degrading work of casting bronze, hewing marble into shape, and painting forms on the wall.

He professed admiration for the manners of the ancient times, and vaunted at every opportunity the ancestral virtues.

"Men of the stamp of Curius and Fabricius cultivated their lettuce-beds, and slept under thatched roofs," he said. "They wot of no other statue than the Priapus carved in the heart of a box-tree, who, protruding his vigorous pale in the centre of their garden, threatened pilferers with a terrible and shameful punishment."

Mela, who was well versed in the annals of Rome, opposed to this opinion the example of an old patrician.

"In the days of the Republic," he pointed out, "that illustrious man, Caius Fabius, of a family issued from Hercules and Evander, limned with his own hand on the walls of the Temple of Salus paintings so highly prized that their recent loss, on the destruction of the temple by fire, has been considered a public misfortune. It is moreover related that he did not doff his toga when painting, thus to indicate that such work was not unworthy of a Roman citizen. He was given the surname of Pictor, which his descendants were proud to bear."

Lucius Cassius replied with vivacity:

"When painting victories in a temple, Caius Fabius had in mind those victories, and not the painting of them. No painters existed in Rome in those days. Anxious that the doughty deeds of his ancesters should for ever be present to the gaze of the Romans, he set an example to the artisans. But just as a pontiff or an ædile lays the first stone of an edifice, without exercising for that the trade of a mason or of an architect, Caius Fabius executed the first painting Rome boasted of, without it being permissible to number him with the workmen who earn their livelihood by painting on walls."

Apollodorus signified approval of this speech with a nod, and, stroking his philosophic beard, remarked:

"The sons of Ascanius are born to rule the world. Any other care would be unworthy of them."

Then, speaking at some length and in well-rounded sentences, he sang the praises of the Romans. He flattered them because he feared them. But in his innermost being, he felt nothing but contempt for their shallow intelligences so devoid of finesse. He beslavered Gallio with praise in these words:

"Thou hast ornamented this city with magnificent monuments. Thou hast assured the liberty of its Senate and of its people. Thou hast decreed excellent regulations for trade and navigation, and thou dispensest justice with even tempered equity. Thy statue shall stand in the Forum. The title shall be granted to you of the second founder of Corinth, or rather Corinth shall take from you the name of Annæa. All these things are worthy of a Roman, and worthy of Gallio. But, do not think that the Greeks have an exaggerated affection for the manual arts. If many of them are engaged in painting vases, in dyeing stuffs, and in modelling figures, it is through necessity. Ulysses constructed his bed and his ship with his own hands. At the same time, the Greeks proclaim that it is unworthy of a wise man to give himself up to futile and gross

arts. In his youth, Socrates followed the trade of a
sculptor, and modelled an image of the Charites still
to be seen on the Acropolis of Athens. His skill
was certainly not of a mediocre order, and, had he
so wished, he could, like the most renowed artists,
have portrayed an athlete throwing a discus or
bandaging his head. But he abandoned like works
to devote himself to the quest of wisdom, as com-
manded by the oracle. Henceforth, he attached
himself to young men, not for the purpose of meas-
uring the proportions of their bodies but solely to
teach them that which is honest. He preferred
those whose soul was beautiful to those of perfect
form, differing in this respect from sculptors, painters and debauchees, who consider only external
beauty, despising the inner comeliness. You are
aware that Phidias engraved on the great toe of his
Jupiter the name of an athlete, because he was
handsome, and without considering whether he was
pure."

"Hence it is," was Gallio's summing up, "that
we do not sing the praises of sculptors, while
bestowing them on their works."

"By Hercules!" exclaimed Lollius, "I do not
know whether to admire most that Venus or that
Faun. The goddess seems to reflect coolness from
the water still dripping from her. She is truly the
desire of gods and men; do you not fear, Gallio,
that some night, a lout concealed in your grounds

may subject her to an outrage similar to the one inflicted by a profane youth, so it is reported, on the Aphrodite of the Cnidians? The priestesses of her temple discovered one morning traces of the outrage on the body of the goddess, and travellers affirm that from that day until now she bears the indelible mark of her defilement. The audacity of the man and the patience of the Immortal One are to be wondered at."

"The crime did not remain unpunished," affirmed Gallio. "The sacrilegious profaner flung himself into the sea, and fell on the rocks a shapeless mass. He was never again seen."

"There can be no doubt," resumed Lollius, "that the Venus of Cnidus surpasses all others in beauty. But the artisan who carved the one in your grounds, Gallio, knew how to make marble plastic. Look at that Faun; he is laughing, and saliva moistens his teeth and his lips; his cheeks have the fresh bloom of the apple: his whole body glistens with youth. However, I prefer the Venus to the Faun."

Raising his right arm, Apollodorus said:

"Most gentle Lollius, just think a bit, and you will fain admit that a like preference is pardonable in an ignorant individual who follows his instincts and who reasons not, but that it is not permitted to one as wise as yourself. That Venus cannot be as beautiful as that Faun, for the body of woman enjoys a perfection lesser than that of man, and the copy of a thing which is less perfect can never equal in beauty the copy of a thing that is more perfect. No doubt can assuredly exist, Lollius, that the body of woman is less beautiful than that of man, since it contains a less beautiful soul. Women are vain, quarrelsome, their mind occupied with trifles and incapable of elevated thoughts, while sickness oftentimes obscures their intellect."

"And yet," remarked Gallio, "both in Rome and in Athens, virgins and matrons have been held worthy of presiding over sacred rites and of placing offerings on the altars. Nay more, the gods have at times selected virgins to give utterance to their oracular words, or to reveal the future to men. Cassandra wore the bands of Apollo about her head and prophesied the discomfiture of the Trojans. Juturna, to whom the love of a god gave immortality, was entrusted with the guardianship of the fountains of Rome."

"Quite true," replied Apollodorus. "But the gods sell dearly to virgins the privilege of interpreting their wishes, and of announcing future events. While conferring on them the power of seeing that which is hidden, they deprive them of their reason and inflict madness on them. I will, however, Gallio, grant you that some women are better than some men and that some men are less good than some women. This arises from the fact that the two sexes are not as distinct and separate from each other as one would believe, and that, quite on the contrary, there is something of man in many women, and of woman in many a man. The following is the explanation of this commingling:

"The ancestors of the men who nowadays people the earth sprang from the hands of Prometheus, who, to give them shape, kneaded the clay as does the potter. He did not confine himself to shaping with his hands a single couple. Far too prudent and too industrious to cause the entire human race to grow from one seed and from a single vessel, he undertook the manufacture of a multitude of women and men, in order to secure at once to humanity the advantage of numbers. In order better to carry out so difficult a work, he modelled separately at the outset all the parts which were to constitute both male and female bodies. He fashioned as many lungs, livers, hearts, brains, bladders, spleens, intestines, matrices and generative organs as were required, and, lastly, he made with subtle art, and in sufficient quantity, all the organs by means of which human beings might breathe freely, feed themselves, and enjoy the reproduction of the species. He forgot neither muscles, tendons, bones, blood nor fluids. He next cut out skins, intending to place in each one, as in a sack, the requisite articles. All these component parts of men and women were duly finished, and nothing remained but to put them together, when he was of a sudden invited to partake of supper at the residence of Bacchus. He went thither, crowned with roses, and indulged too freely in libations to the god, returning with tottering steps to his workshop. His brain befogged with the fumes of wine, his eyesight dimmed, and his hands shaky, he resumed his task, greatly to our misfortune. The distribution of organs among human beings seemed to him an easy enough pastime. He knew not what he was about, and was perfectly contented with his job, however badly he accomplished it. He was constantly and inadvertently allotting to woman that which was proper to man, and to man the things pertaining to woman.

"Thus it came about that our first parents were composed of ill-assorted pieces which did not harmonise. And, having mated by choice or at haphazard, they produced beings as incoherent as themselves. Thus has it come about, through the Titan's fault, that we see so many virile women and so many effeminate men. This also explains the contradictory characteristics to be met with in the firmest of minds and how it is that the most determined character is perpetually false to itself. And, finally, this is why we are all at variance with our own selves."

Lucius Cassius expressed condemnation of this

fable, because it did not teach man to conquer himself, but on the contrary induced him to yield to nature.

Gallio pointed out that the poets and philosophers gave a different interpretation as to the origin of the world and the creation of mankind.

"The fables told by the Greeks," he said, "should not be believed in too blindly, nor should we hold as truthful, Apollodorus, what they state in particular concerning the stones thrown by Pyrrha. The philosophers are in accord among themselves as to the principle presiding over the creation of the world, and leave us in doubt as to whether the earth was produced by water, by air, or, as seems more credible, by the subtile heat. But the Greeks wish to know all things, and so they forge ingenious falsehood. How much better it is to confess our ignorance. The past is as much concealed from us as is the future; we are circumscribed by two dense clouds, in the forgetfulness of what was, and in the uncertainty of what shall be. And yet we suffer ourselves to be the playthings of an inquisitive desire to become acquainted with the causes of things, and a consuming anxiety incites us to ponder over the destinies of mankind and of the world."

"It is true," sighed Cassius, "that we are everlastingly striving to penetrate the impenetrable future. We toil at this quest with all our might, and call to our aid all kinds of means. Anon we think to attain our object by meditation; again, by prayer and ecstasy. Some of us consult the oracles of the gods; others, fearing not to do that which is forbidden, appeal to the augurs of Chaldæa, or try the Babylonian spells. Futile and sacrilegious curiosity! For, of what advantage would be to us the knowledge of future things, since they are inevitable! Nevertheless the wise men, still more so than the vulgar herd, feel the desire of delving into the future and of, so to speak, hurling themselves into it. It is doubtless because they hope thus to escape the present which inflicts on them so much that is sad and distasteful. Why should not the men of to-day be goaded with the desire of fleeing from these wretched times? We are living in an age replete with deeds of cowardice, abounding in ignominious acts, and fertile in crimes."

Cassius spoke at some length in depreciation of the times in which he lived. He lamented the fact that the Romans, fallen from their ancient virtues, no longer found any pleasure except in the consumption of the oysters of the Lucrine lake and of the birds of Phasis river, and that they had no taste except for mummers, chariot-drivers, and gladiators. He deplored the ills which the Empire was suffering from, the insolent luxury of the great, the contemptible avidity of the clients, and the savage depravity of the multitude.

Gallio and his brother agreed with him. They

loved virtue. Nevertheless, they had nothing in
common with the patricians of old who, having no
other care than the fattening of their swine, and the
performance of the sacred rites, conquered the
world for the better administration of their farms.
This nobility of the byre, instituted by Romulus and
Remus, was long since extinct. The patrician
families created by the divine Julius and by the
Emperor Augustus, had passed away. Intelligent
men from all the provinces of the Empire had
stepped into their places. Romans in Rome, they
were nowhere strangers. They greatly surpassed
the old Cethegus family by their refined minds and
humane feelings. They did not regret the Republic;
they did not regret liberty, the recollection of which
recalled simultaneously proscriptions and civil wars.
They honoured Cato as the heroic figure of another
age, without wishing to see so exalted a type of
virtue arise on top of fresh ruins. They looked
upon the Augustan epoch and the first years of
Tiberius as the happiest the world had ever known,
since the Golden Age had existed in the imagination
of the poets only. They lamented the fact that the
new order of things, which had promised the world
a long reign of felicity, should have so promptly
burdened Rome with an unheard of shame unknown
even to the contemporaries of Marius and Sulla.
They had, during the madness of Caius, seen the
best citizens branded with a hot iron, sentenced to

the mines, to labour on the roads, thrown to wild beasts, fathers compelled to be present at the agony of their children, and men shining by their virtues, such as Cremutius Cordus, suffer themselves to die of starvation, in order to cheat the tyrant of their death. To Rome's shame, be it said, Caligula respected neither his sisters nor the most illustrious dames. And, what filled these rhetors and philosophers with as great an indignation as the one they felt over the rape of the matrons and the assassination of the best citizens, were the crimes perpetrated by Caius against eloquence and letters. This madman had conceived the idea of destroying the poems of Homer, and had caused to be removed from all bookshelves the writings, the portraits, and the names of Virgil and of Livy. Finally, Gallio could not forgive him for having compared the style of Seneca to mortar without cement.

They dreaded Claudius in a somewhat lesser degree, but despised him the more for all that. They ridiculed his pumpkin-like head and his seal-like voice. That old savant was not a monster of wickedness. The worst they could reproach him with was his weakness. But, in the exercise of the sovereign power, such weakness became at times as cruel as the cruelty of Caius. They also bore domestic grievances against him. If Caius had held Seneca up to ridicule, Claudius had banished him to Corsica. It is true that he had subsequently re-

called him to Rome and conferred a prætorship on
him. But they showed him no gratitude for
having thus carried out the behests of Agrippina, in
ignorance of what he was commanding. Indignant
but long suffering, they left it to the Empress to
determine the fate of the aged man, and the choice
of the new prince. Many rumours were current
to the shame of the unchaste and cruel daughter of
Germanicus. They heeded them not, and sang the
praises of the illustrious woman to whom the
Senecas owed the termination of their misfortune
and their rise in honours. As will oftentimes
happen, their convictions were in harmony with
their interests. A painful experience of public life
had left unshaken their trust in the *régime* established by the divine Augustus, a *régime* placed on a
firmer basis by Tiberius, and under which they filled
high positions. They were reckoning on a new
master to redress the evils engendered by the
masters of the Empire.

Gallio produced from the folds of his toga a roll
of papyrus.

"Dear friends," he said, "I have learnt this
morning, through letters from Rome, that our
young prince has married Octavia, the daughter of
Cæsar."

A murmur of approval greeted the news.

"We should indeed," continued Gallio, "congratulate ourselves over a union, by virtue of which

the prince, combining with his former qualifications those of husband and of son-in-law, becomes henceforth the equal of Britannicus. My brother Seneca never ceases praising in his letters to me the eloquence and gentleness of his pupil who sheds lustre on his youth by pleading before the Senate in the presence of the Emperor. He has not yet completed his sixteenth year, yet he has already won the cases of three unfortunate or guilty cities—Ilion, Bolonia, and Apamea."

"He has not then," asked Lucius Cassius, "inherited the evil disposition of the Domitians, his ancestors?"

"Indeed he has not," replied Gallio. "It is Germanicus who lives anew in him."

Annæus Mela, who was not looked upon as a sycophant, joined in the praise of the son of Agrippina. His praises appeared affecting and sincere, since he pledged them, so to speak, on the head of his son, who was still of tender age.

"Nero is chaste, modest, of a kindly disposition, and religious. My little Lucan, who is dearer to me than my eyes, was his play- and school-mate. Together they practised declamation in the Greek and Latin languages. Together they attempted to indite verse. Never did Nero, in the course of these contests of skill at versification, manifest the slightest symptom of jealousy. Quite the contrary, he enjoyed praising his rival's verses, which, in spite of his tender age, revealed traces here and there of a consuming energy. He sometimes seemed happy to be surpassed by the nephew of his teacher. Such was the charming modesty of the prince of youth! Poets will some day compare the friendship of Nero and Lucan with that of Euryalus and Nisus."

"Nero," the proconsul went on to say, "displays with the ardour of youth a gentle and merciful spirit. Time will but strengthen such virtues.

"Claudius, when adopting him, has wisely acquiesced in the hope expressed by the Senate and the wish of the people. In so doing, he has removed from the Imperial succession a child overwhelmed by the shame of his mother, and has now, by giving Octavia to Nero, secured the accession of a youthful Cæsar whom Rome will delight in. The respectful son of an honoured mother, the zealous disciple of a philosopher, Nero, whose adolescence is illumined with the most agreeable qualities, Nero, our hope and the hope of the world, will remember, when clad in purple, the teachings of the Portico, and will rule the universe with justice and moderation."

"We welcome the omen," remarked Lollius. "May an era of happiness dawn upon the human race!"

" 'Tis difficult to predict the future," said Gallio. "Still, we experience no doubts regarding the eternity of the City. The oracles have promised Rome an empire without end, and it would be sacrilegious not to put our faith in the gods. Shall I reveal to you my fondest hope? I joyfully expect the time when peace will reign for ever on the earth, following upon the chastising of the Parthians. Yes indeed, we may, without fear of deceiving ourselves, herald the end of war so hated by mothers. Who is there to disturb the Roman peace henceforth? Our eagles have spread to the confines of the universe. All the nations have experienced our strength and our mercy. The Arab, the Sabæan, the dweller on the slopes of the Hæmus, the Sarmatian who quenches his thirst with the blood of his steed, the Sygambri of the curly locks, the woolly-headed Ethiopian, all come in hordes to worship Rome their protectress. Whence would new barbarians spring? Is it likely that the icy plains of the North or the burning sands of Libya hold in store enemies of the Roman nation? All Barbarians, won over to our friendship, will lay down their arms, and Rome, the white-haired great-grandmother, tranquil in her old age, will see the nations respectfully grouped about her as her adopted children, dwelling in harmony and love."

All signified their approval of the foregoing sentiments, excepting Cassius, who shook his head in disagreement.

He felt a pride in his military ancestry while the glory of arms, so greatly extolled by poets and rhetors, kindled his enthusiasm.

"I doubt, my friend Gallio," he commented, "that nations will ever cease to hate and fear one another. To tell the truth, I should not desire such a consummation. Did war cease, what would become of strength of character, grandeur of soul, and love of country? Courage and devotion would be virtues out of date."

"Rest assured, Lucius," said Gallio, "that when men shall cease to conquer one another, they will strive to subdue their own selves. That is the most virtuous attempt they can make, and the most noble use to which they can put their bravery and magnanimity. Yes, indeed, the august mother whose wrinkles and whose hairs, blanched by centuries, we worship, Rome, will establish universal peace. Then shall the enjoyment of life be realised. Life under certain conditions is worth living. Life is a tiny flame between two infinite shadows; 'tis our share of the divine essence. During the term of his life, a man is similar to the gods."

While Gallio was thus discoursing, a dove perched itself on the shoulder of Venus, whose marble contours gleamed among the myrtles.

"My dear Gallio," said Lollius with a smile, "the bird of Aphrodite takes delight in thy words. They are gentle and full of gracefulness."

A slave approached, bearing cool wine, and the friends of the proconsul discoursed of the gods. Apollodorus was of opinion that it was not easy to grasp their nature. Lollius doubted their very existence.

"When thunder peals," he said, "it all depends upon the philosopher whether it is the cloud or the god who has thundered."

Cassius, however, did not countenance such thoughtless arguments. He believed in the gods of the Republic. While entertaining doubts as to the extent of their providence, he asserted their existence, as he did not wish to differ from humanity on an essential point. And to support his belief in the faith of his ancestors, he had recourse to an argument he had learnt from the Greeks.

"The gods exist," he said. "Men have formed their idea of what they are like. Now, it is impossible to conceive an image not based on reality. How would it be possible to see Minerva, Neptune, and Mercury, were there neither Mercury, nor Neptune, nor Minerva?"

"You have convinced me," said Lollius mockingly. "The old woman who sells honey-cakes in the Forum, outside the basilica, has seen the god Typhon, he with the shaggy head of an ass, and a monster belly. He threw her on her back, threw her clothes over her ears, chastised her while keeping time to each resounding blow, and left her for dead, after polluting her in a disgusting fashion. She has herself told how, even as Antiope, she had been favoured with the visit of an immortal god. It is certain that the god Typhon exists, since he committed an outrage on an old cake-selling hag."

"In spite of thy mockery, Marcus, I do not doubt the existence of the gods," resumed Cassius. "And I believe that they enjoy a human form, since it is under that form that they always show themselves to us, whether we slumber or whether we are awake."

"It would be better," remarked Apollodorus, "to say that men possess the divine form, since the gods existed before them."

"My dear Apollodorus," exclaimed Lollius. "You forget that Diana was first worshipped under the form of a tree, and that several important gods have the shape of an unhewn stone. Cybele is represented, not as a woman should be, with two breasts, but with several teats like a bitch or a sow. The sun is a god, but being too hot to assume the human form, he has taken the shape of a ball; he is a round god."

Annæus Mela gently censured this academic jesting.

"All that is related about the gods," he said, should not be taken literally. The vulgar herd calls wheat Ceres, and wine Bacchus. But where is to be found the man crazy enough to believe that

he drinks and eats a god? Let us indulge in a
more exalted knowledge of the divine nature. The
gods are but the several parts of nature, and they
are all lost in one god, who is nature in its entirety."

The proconsul signified his approval of the words
of his brother, and speaking in a serious strain,
defined the attributes of divinity.

"God is the soul of the world; this soul spreads
to all parts of the universe, infusing motion and
life into it. This soul, a creative flame, penetrating
the inert mass of matter, gave shape to the world,
governing and preserving it. Divinity, an active
force, is essentially good. The matter which it has
put to good use, being inert and passive, is bad in
certain of its parts. God has been powerless to
change its nature. This explains the origin of the
evil in the world. Our souls are particles of the
divine fire into which they will some day be merged.
Consequently, God is within us and he dwells in
particular in the virtuous man whose soul is not
hampered with gross materialism. This wise man,
in whom God dwells, is God's equal. He should
not implore him, but contain him within himself.
And what madness it is to pray to God! What an
act of impiety it is to petition him! It is tanta-
mount to believe that it is possible to enlighten his
intelligence, to change his heart, and to persuade
him to mend his behaviour. It is displaying
ignorance of the necessity governing his immutable

wisdom. He is subjected to Destiny, or, to be more accurate, he is Destiny. His ways are laws to which he is like ourselves subjected. For once that he commands, he obeys for ever. Free and powerful in his submission, it is to himself that he shows obedience. All the happenings in the world are the manifestations of sovereign intentions originating with himself. His helplessness against himself is infinite."

Gallio's speech was applauded by his hearers. Apollodorus, however, craved permission to submit a few objections.

"You are right, Gallio," he said, "when you believe that Jupiter is at the mercy of Anankè and I hold with you that Anankè is the first among the immortal goddesses. But it appears to me that your god, above all admirable in his compass and his perpetuity, had better intentions than luck when he created the world, since he found nothing better wherewith to knead it than a rebellious and ingrate substance, and that the material betrays the workman. I cannot but feel for him over his discomfiture. The potters of Athens are more fortunate. They procure, for the purpose of making vases, a delicate and plastic clay which readily takes and preserves the contours they give it. Hence do their goblets and amphoræ present an agreeable form. Their curves are graceful, and the painter limns with ease figures pleasing to the eye, such as old

Silenus bestriding his ass, the toilet of Aphrodite,
and the chaste Amazons.   When I come to think of
it, Gallio, I am of the opinion that if your god was
less fortunate than the potters of Athens, 'tis for the
reason that he lacked wisdom and that he was a
poor artisan.   The material at his disposal was not
of the best.   Still, it was not devoid of all service-
able properties, as you have yourself confessed.
Nothing is absolutely good or absolutely bad.   A
thing may be bad if put to a certain use, while it
may be excellent in some other.   It would be waste
of time to plant olive-trees in the clay used in
fashioning amphoræ.   The tree of Pallas would not
grow in the light and pure soil of which are made
the beautiful vases which our victorious athletes
receive, blushing the while with pride and modesty.
It seems to me, Gallio, that your god, when fashioning the world with a material that was not suitable
for the undertaking, was guilty of the mistake which
a vine-dresser of Megara would be committing, were
he to plant a vine in modelling clay, or were some
worker in ceramics to select for the making of
amphoræ the stony soil which affords nutriment to
the clusters of the grape-vine.   Your god, you say,
made the universe.   He ought certainly to have
given form to some other thing, in order to make
suitable use of his material.   Since the substance, as
you assert, proved rebellious to him, either through
its inherent inertia, or through some other bad qual-

ity, should he have persisted in putting it to a use it could not respond to, and, as the saying goes, carve his bow out of a cypress? The secret of industry does not consist in accomplishing much, but in doing good work. Why did he not content himself with creating some small thing, say a gnat, or a drop of water, but finish it to perfection?

"I might add further remarks about your god, Gallio, and ask you, for instance, if you do not entertain a fear that from his constant rubbing against matter, he may wear out, just as a millstone becomes worn in the long run in the course of grinding wheat. But such questions are not to be solved in a hurry, and the time of a proconsul is precious. Permit me at least to say to you that you are not justified in believing that your god rules and preserves the world, since, according to your own admission, he deprived himself of intelligence after having become acquainted with all things; of will-power, after having willed all things, and of power, following upon his ability to do what he saw fit. Herein again lay, on his part, a serious mistake, for he was thus an instrument in depriving himself of the means of correcting his imperfect work. So far as I am concerned, I am inclined to believe that god is in reality, not the one you have conceived, but indeed the matter he discovered on a certain day, and which the Greeks have styled chaos. You are mistaken in your belief that matter is inert. It is ever in motion, and its perpetual activity keeps life a-going throughout the universe."

Thus spake the philosopher Apollodorus. Gallio, who had listened to his speech with some degree of impatience, denied that he had fallen a victim to the mistakes and contradictions with which the Greek charged him. But he failed in refuting successfully the arguments of his opponent, as his intellect was not a subtle one and because he demanded principally of philosophy the means of rendering men virtuous, and because he was interested in useful truths only.

"Try to grasp, Apollodorus," he said, "that God is none other than nature. Nature and himself are one. God and Nature are the two names of a single being, just as Novatus and Gallio designate one and the same man. God, if you prefer, is divine reason commingling with the earth. You need have no fear that he will wear out through this amalgamation, since his tenous substance participates of the fire which consumes all matter while remaining unchanged.

"But should, nevertheless," proceeded Gallio, "my doctrine embrace ill-assorted ideas, do not blame me for it, my dear Apollodorus, but rather give me praise because I suffer a few contradictions to find a place in my mind. Were I not conciliatory as regards my own ideas, were I to confer upon a single system an exclusive preference, I could no

longer tolerate the freedom of every opinion; having destroyed my own freedom of thought, I could
not readily tolerate it in the case of others, and
I should forfeit the respect due to every doctrine
established or professed by a sincere man. The
gods forbid that I should see my opinion prevail to
the exclusion of any other, and exercise an absolute
sway on other minds. Conjure up a picture, my
dear friends, of the state of manners and morals,
were a sufficient number of men firmly to believe
that they were the sole possessors of the truth, if,
by some impossible chance, they were thoroughly
agreed as to that truth. A too narrow piety among
the Athenians, who are nevertheless full of wisdom
and of doubt, was the cause of the banishment of
Anaxagoras and of the death of Socrates. What
would happen were millions of men enslaved by one
solitary idea concerning the nature of the gods?
The genius of the Greeks and the prudence of our
ancestors made allowance for doubt, and tolerated
the worship of Jupiter under several names. No
sooner should a powerful sect come on this ailing
earth and proclaim that Jupiter has one name only,
than blood would flow the world over, and no
longer would there be but one Caius whose madness
should threaten the human race with death. All
the men of such a sect would be so many Caiuses.
They would face death for a name. For a name,
they would kill, since it is rather in the nature of

men to kill than to die on behalf of what seems to them true and most excellent. Hence it is better to base public order on the diversity of opinions, than to seek to establish it on a universal consent to one and the same belief. A like unanimous consent could never be realised, and in seeking to obtain it, men would become stupid and maddened. For, indeed, the most patent truth is but a vain jangle of words to the men on whom it is attempted to impose it. You would compel me to believe a thing which you understand, but which passes my understanding. You would thus be forcing upon me not a thing that is intelligible, but one that is incomprehensible. And I am nearer you when holding a different belief, one which I understand. For, in that case, both of us are making use of our reason, and we both possess an intelligent comprehension of our own belief."

"Enough of all this," remarked Lollius. "Educated men will never combine for the purpose of stifling all other doctrines to the advantage of a single one. As to the vulgar herd, who cares to teach it that Jupiter has six hundred names, or a single one?"

Cassius, slow of utterance, and of a serious turn of mind, spoke next.

"Beware, Gallio," he said, "lest the existence of God, such as expounded by you, be not in contradiction with the beliefs of our forefathers. It matters little, after all, whether your arguments are better or worse than those of Apollodorus. What we have to consider is the fatherland. To its religion does Rome owe her virtues and her power. To destroy our gods is to compass our own destruction."

"You need not fear, my friend," rejoined Gallio with some show of animation, "have no fear, I repeat, that I deny in an insolent spirit the heavenly protectors of the Empire. The only divinity which the philosophers acknowledge embodies within itself all the gods, just as humanity embraces all men. The gods whose worship was instituted by the wisdom of our forefathers, Jupiter, Juno, Mars, Minerva, Quirinus, and Hercules, constitute the most august parts of the universal providence, and no less than the whole do these parts exist. No, indeed, I am not an impious man, nor inimical to the laws. None respects the sacred things more than Gallio."

No one seemed disposed to dispute these ideas. Thereupon Lollius, bringing the conversation back to its starting-point, remarked:

"We have been seeking to penetrate the veil of the future. What are man's destinies, according to you, my friends, after his demise?"

In reply to this question, Annæus Mela promised immortality to heroes and wise men, while denying it to the common of mankind.

"It passes belief," he said, "that misers, gluttons, and mean-spirited men should possess an immortal soul. Could so singular a privilege be the portion of coarse and silly oafs? I cannot entertain such a thought. It would be an insult to the majority of the gods to believe that they have decreed the immortality of the boor who wots only of his goats and cheeses, or of the freedman richer than Crœsus, who had no other cares in the world than to check the accounts of his stewards. Why, good gods, should they be provided with a soul? What sort of a figure would they present among heroes and wise men in the Elysian fields? These wretches, like so many others here below, are incapable of realising humanity's short-spanned life. How could they realise a life of longer duration? Vulgar souls are snuffed out at the hour of death, or they may for a while whirl about our globe, to vanish in the dense strata of the atmosphere. Virtue only, by making man the equal of the gods, makes them participate in their immortality. To quote the poet:

" 'Illustrious virtue never descends into the Stygian shades. Lead a hero's life, and the fates will not consign thee to the pitiless river of forgetfulness. When comes thy last day, glory will open to thee the path of heaven.'

"Let us realise our condition. We must all die, and all that we are must die. The man of shining virtue simply escapes the common destiny by be-

coming god, and by obtaining his admission into
Olympus among the Heroes and the Gods."

"But he is not conscious of his own apotheosis,"
said Marcus Lollius. "There does not exist upon
earth a slave or a barbarian who is not aware that
Augustus is a god. But Augustus knows it not.
Hence it is that our Cæsars journey reluctantly
towards the constellations, and even now we see
Claudius near with blanched face these shadowy
honours."

Gallio shook his head, and remarked, "The poet
Euripides has said:

" 'We love the life which is revealed unto us upon earth,
since we know of no other.'

"Everything that is related concerning the dead
is open to doubt, and is bound up with fables and
falsehoods. Nevertheless, I believe that virtuous
men attain an immortality of which they are fully
cognisant. Let it be clearly understood that they
achieve it by their own efforts, and not as a recom-
pense conferred by the gods. By what right should
the immortal gods degrade a virtuous man to the
extent of rewarding him? The leading of a blame-
less life is its own reward, and no prize is there
worthy of virtue, which is its own reward. Let us
leave to vulgar souls, that they may thereby sustain
their wretched fortitude, the dread of punishment,
and the hope of a reward. Let us love virtue for

its own sake. Gallio, if what the poets tell of the infernal regions be true, if after your death you are arraigned before the tribunal of Minos, you may say to him: 'Minos shall not judge me. By my actions have I been judged.' "

"How," inquired Apollodorus the philosopher, "can the gods give to men an immortality they themselves do not enjoy?"

Apollodorus, indeed, did not believe in the immortality of the gods, or rather that their sway over the world should be exercised for all time.

He proceeded to develop the reasons for his belief.

"The reign of Jupiter," he said, "began after the Golden Age. We know through the traditions preserved for us by the poets that the son of Saturn succeeded to his father in the governing of the world. Now, everything that had a beginning must have an end. It is foolish to suppose that anything finite in one part can be infinite in another. It would then become necessary to call it finite and infinite as a whole, which would be absurd. Anything possessed of an extreme point can be measured from that point itself, and could not in any way cease to be measured at any point of its extent, without changing its nature, and the proper of what is measurable is to be comprised between two extreme points. We may therefore make up our minds that the reign of Jupiter will end just as did that of Saturn. As Æschylus has said:

" 'Jupitor is subordinate to Anankè. He cannot escape his fate.' "

Gallio thought the same, for reasons derived from the observation of nature.

"I consider with you, Apollodorus, that the reigns of the gods are not immortal, and the observation of the celestial phenomena inclines me to this belief. The heavens, as well as the earth, are subject to corruption, and the divine palaces, liable to ruin just as the dwellings of mankind, crumble under the weight of the centuries.   I have seen stones fall from the aerial regions.   They were blackened and corroded by fire, and bore testimony to a celestial conflagration.

"The bodies of the gods, Apollodorus, are not any more exempt from injury than their dwellings. If it be true, as Homer teaches, that the gods, inhabitants of Olympus, impregnate the flanks of goddesses and mortal women, it is assuredly because they are not themselves immortal, in spite of their life's span being greater than that of mankind, and hence it is patent that fate subjects them to the necessity of transmitting a life which they may not enjoy for ever."

"In truth," said Lollius, "it is hardly to be conceived that immortals should produce children in the same way as human beings and animals, or even that they should possess organs adapted to such a purpose. But perhaps the loves of the gods owe their origin to the mendacity of the poets."

Apollodorus persisted in his assertion that the reign of Jupiter would some day cease, supporting his opinion with subtle reasons. He prophesied that Prometheus would succeed the son of Saturn.

"Prometheus," replied Gallio, "was set free by Hercules with the consent of Jupiter, and he enjoys in Olympus the happiness he owes to his foresight and to his love of mankind. Nothing will ever happen to change his happy fate."

Apollodorus asked him:

"Who then, according to you, Gallio, shall inherit the thunder which sets the world a-quaking?"

"Although it may seem audacious to answer this question," replied Gallio, "I think I am competent to do so, and to name Jove's successor."

As he spoke, an officer of the basilica, whose duty it was to call cases, approached him, and informed him that some suitors were waiting for him in court.

The proconsul asked if the matter was one of paramount importance.

"It is a most petty case, Gallio," replied the officer of the basilica. "A man from the harbour of Cenchreæ has just dragged a stranger before your tribunal. They are both Jews and of humble condition. They are quarrelling over some barbarian custom or some gross superstition, as is the wont of Syrians. Here is the minute of their case. It is all Punic to the clerk who wrote it.

"The plaintiff sets forth, Gallio, that he is the head of the assembly of the Jews or, as one says in Greek, of the synagogue, and he begs justice of you against a man from Tarsus, who, recently settled at Cenchreæ, goes every Sunday to the synagogue, for the purpose of speaking against the Jewish law. 'It is a scandal and an abomination, which thou shalt put an end to,' says the plaintiff, and he clamours for the integrity of the privileges belonging to the children of Israel. The defendant claims for all those who believe his teachings adoption and incorporation into the family of a man named Abraham, and he threatens the plaintiff with the divine fire. You see, Gallio, that the case is a petty and ambiguous one. It rests with you to decide whether you will take the case yourself, or whether you will leave it to be judged by a lesser magistrate."

The proconsul's friends begged him not to disturb himself for so miserable an affair.

"I make it my duty," he said in response to their prayers, "to follow in this respect the rules laid down by the divine Augustus. I must therefore try personally, not only important cases, but also smaller ones, when the jurisprudence concerning them has not been determined. Certain light cases recur daily and are of importance, if only for their frequency. It is meet that I should personally try one of each class. A judgment rendered by a proconsul serves as an example, and establishes a precedent in law."

"You deserve praise, Gallio," said Lollius, "for the zeal you display in the fulfilment of your consular duties. But, acquainted as I am with your wisdom, I doubt whether it is agreeable for you to render justice. That which men honour with this title is really an administration of base prudence and of cruel revenge. Human laws are the daughters of fear and anger."

Gallio protested feebly against this definition. He did not admit that human laws bore the character of real justice, saying:

"The punishment of crime consists in its commission. The penalty added thereto by the laws is superfluous, and does not fit the crime. However, since through the fault of mankind laws there are, we should apply them equitably."

Thereupon he told the officer of the court that he would proceed to the tribunal very shortly, and, turning towards his friends, he said:

"To speak truly, I have a special reason for looking into this case with my own eyes. I must not neglect any opportunity of keeping an eye on these Jews of Cenchreæ, a turbulent, rancorous race, which shows contempt for the laws, and which it is

not easy to hold in check. If ever the peace of
Corinth should be troubled, it will be by them.
This port, where all the ships of the East come to
anchor, conceals amid a congested mass of warehouses and taverns, a countless horde of thieves,
eunuchs, soothsayers, sorcerers, lepers, desecraters
of graves, and assassins. It is the haunt of every
abomination and of every form of superstition.
Isis, Eschmoun, the Phœnician Venus, and the god
of the Jews, are all worshipped there. I am
alarmed at seeing those unclean Jews multiply,
rather in the way of fishes than in that of mankind.
They swarm about the miry streets of the harbour
like crabs under the rocks."

"What is more dreadful is that they infest Rome
to a like extent," exclaimed Lucius Cassius. "To
great Pompey's own door must be laid the
crime of introducing this plague of leprosy into the
City. He it was who committed the wrong of not
treating as did our ancestors the prisoners he
brought from Judæa for his triumphal entry into
the City, and they have peopled the right bank of
the Tiber with their base spawn. Dwelling about
the base of the Janiculum, amid the tanneries, the
gut-works, and the fermenting-troughs, in the suburbs whither flock all the abominations and horrors
of the world, they earn their livelihood at the
vilest of trades, unloading lighters, selling rags
and refuse, and exchanging matches for broken

glasses. Their women tell fortunes in the houses of the wealthy; their children beg from the frequenters of Egeria's groves. As you rightly said, Gallio, hostile to the human race and to themselves, they are ever fomenting sedition. A few years back, the followers of a certain Chrestus or Cherestus raised bloody riots among the Jews. The Porta Portuensis was put to fire and sword, and Cæsar was compelled to exercise severe repression, in spite of his forbearance. He expelled from Rome the leaders of the movement."

"Full well do I know it," said Gallio. "Several of these exiles came to Cenchreæ, among others a Jew and a Jewess from the Pontus, who still dwell there, following some humble trade. I believe that they weave the coarse stuffs of Cilicia. I have not learnt anything noteworthy in regard to the partisans of Chrestus. As to Chrestus himself, I am ignorant of what has become of him, and whether he is still of this world."

"I am as ignorant on this score as you are, Gallio," resumed Lucius Cassius, "and no one will ever know it. These vile wretches do not so much as attain celebrity in the annals of crime. Moreover, there are so many slaves of the name of Chrestus that it would be no easy matter to distinguish a particular one amid the throng.

"It is but a trifling matter that the Jews should cause tumult within the low purlieus where their

number and their lowliness protect them from
supervision. They swarm through the city, they
ingratiate themselves into families, and are everywhere a source of trouble. They shout in the
Forum on behalf of the agitators who pay them,
and these despicable foreigners incite the citizens to
a hatred of one another. Too long have we endured their presence in popular assemblages, and
for a long time now have public speakers avoided
running counter to the opinion of these wretches,
for fear of their insults. Obstinate in the observance of their barbarian law, they wish to subject others to it, and they find adepts among the
Asiatics, and even among the Greeks. And, what
is hardly to be credited, they impose their customs
on the Latins themselves. There are, in the City,
whole quarters where all the shops are closed on
their Sabbath day. Oh the shame of Rome! And,
while corrupting the lowly folk among whom they
dwell, their kings, admitted into Cæsar's palace, in-
solently practice their superstitions, and set to all
citizens a detestable and noted example. Thus do
the Jews inoculate Italy on all sides with an
oriental venom."

Annæus Mela, who had travelled over the whole
of the Roman world, sought to make his friends
realise the extent of the evil they deplored.

"The Jews corrupt the whole world," he said.
"There is not a Greek city, there are hardly any

barbarian towns where work does not cease on the seventh day, where lamps are not lit, where their keeping of fast-days is not followed, and where the abstaining from the flesh of certain animals is not observed in imitation of them.

"I have met in Alexandria an aged Jew not lacking in intelligence, who was even versed in Greek literature. He rejoiced at the progress of his religion in the Empire. 'In proportion to the knowledge foreigners acquire of our laws,' he told me, 'do they find them pleasant, and they conform readily to them, both Romans and Greeks, those who dwell on the mainland and the people of the isles, Eastern and Western nations, Europe and Asia.' The ancient one spoke perhaps with some degree of exaggeration. Still one sees a number of Greeks yielding to the beliefs of the Jews."

Apollodorus sharply denied such to be the case.

"The Greeks who judaise," he said, "are not to be met with except amid the dregs of the populace. and among the barbarians wandering about Greece, as brigands and tramps. The followers of the Stammerer may, however, have persuaded some few ignorant Greeks, by inducing them to believe that the ideas of Plato are to be found in the Hebrew scriptures. Such is the lie which they strive to spread."

"It is a fact," replied Gallio, "that the Jews recognise an only, invisible, almighty god, who has

created the earth. But they are far from worship-
ping him with wisdom. They publicly proclaim
that this god is the enemy of all that is not Jewish,
and that he will not tolerate in his temple either the
effigies of the other gods, or the statue of Cæsar, or
his own images. They regard as impious those who
fashion out of perishable matter a god the image of
man. Various reasons, some of them good and in
harmony with the ideas which we conceive in regard
to the divine providence, are adduced why this god
should not be given expression to in marble or in
bronze. But what can be thought, dear Apollodorus, of a god sufficiently inimical to the Republic
that he will not admit in his sanctuary the statues
of the Prince? How conceive a god who takes
offence at the honours rendered to other gods?
And what opinion can one have of a nation which
credits its gods with like sentiments! The Jews
look upon the gods of the Latins, Greeks and
Barbarians as hostile gods, and they carry superstition to the point of believing that they possess a
full and complete knowledge of God, one to which
nothing can be added, and from which nothing can
be subtracted.

"As you are aware, my dear friends, it is not
sufficient to tolerate every religion; we should
honour them all, believe that all are sacred, that
they are all coequal in the sincerity of those pro-
fessing them, and that similar to arrows shot from

various points towards the same goal, they all meet
in the bosom of God. Alone the religion which
only tolerates itself, cannot be endured. Were it to
be permitted to spread, it would absorb all others.
Nay, so unsociable a religion is not a religion, but
rather an abligion, and no longer a bond that
unites pious men, but one severing that sacred bond.
It is the most impious of things. Can, indeed, a
greater insult be offered to the deity than to worship
it under a particular form, while at one and the
same time dooming it to execration under all the
other forms it assumes in the eyes of men?

"What! Because I sacrifice to Jupiter crowned
with a bushel, I am to forbid a foreigner from
sacrificing to a Jupiter whose head of hair, similar
to the flower of the hyacinth, drops uncrowned over
his shoulders; and that, impious man that I should
be, I should still consider myself a worshipper of
Jupiter! No, by all means no! The religious man
bound to the immortal gods is equally bound to all
men by the religion which embraces both the earth
and the heavens. Odious is the error of the Jews
who believe they are pious in that they worship their
god alone!"

"They suffer themselves to be circumcised in his
honour," spoke Annæus Mela. "In order that
this mutilation should not be noticed, it is necessary,
when frequenting the public baths, for them to conceal that which should neither be made a display of,

nor covered as a thing of shame. For it is alike ridiculous for a man to pride himself on, or to be ashamed of, what he shares in common with all men. We have good cause to dread, my friends, the progress of Judaic customs in the Empire. There is, however, no cause to fear that Romans and Greeks will adopt circumcision. It passes belief that this custom is likely to make its way among the Barbarians who, however, would feel the disgrace of it to a lesser degree, since they are, for the greater part, absurd enough to reckon as disgraceful for a man to appear before his fellow men in a state of nudity."

"While I think of it!" exclaimed Lollius. "When our gentle Canidia, the flower of the matrons of the Esquiline, sends her beautiful slaves to the hot baths, she compels them to wear drawers, as she grudges everybody even a view of what is most dear to her about their bodies. By Pollux, she will be the cause of their being taken for Jews, an insulting supposition, even for a slave."

Lucius Cassius resumed, revealing the irritation which consumed him:

"I cannot say whether the Jewish folly will overtake the whole world. But it is past endurance that this madness should spread among the ignorant, that it should be tolerated in the Empire, that this fœtid race, which has descended to every form of turpitude, absurd and sordid in its manners and customs, impious and villainous in its laws, and execrated by the immortal gods, should be suffered to exist. The obscene Syrian is corrupting the City of Rome. We have cast aside with contempt our ancient usages, and the salutary methods of discipline of our ancestors. We no longer serve these masters of the earth, who conquered it for us. Which of us still believes in the haruspices? Who is there with any respect for the augurs? Who shows reverence to Mars and the divine Twins? Oh the sad neglect of our religious duties! Italy has repudiated her indigenous gods, and her tutelary genii. She is henceforth on all sides at the mercy of foreign superstitions, and is handed over defenceless to the impure horde of oriental priests. Alas, did Rome conquer the world only to be conquered by the Jews? Warnings have assuredly not been lacking. The overflowing of the Tiber and the grain famine are certainly not doubtful manifestations of the divine ire. No day passes without its sinister presage. The earth quakes, the sun is veiled, while lightning flashes in a clear sky. Wonders follow upon wonders. Birds of ill omen have been seen to perch on the summit of the Capitol. An ox has been heard to speak on the Etruscan shore. Women have brought forth monsters; a wailing voice has sounded amid the recreations of the theatre. The statue of Victory has dropped the reins of her chariot."

"The hosts of the celestial palaces," remarked Lollius, "have strange ways of making themselves heard. If they desire a little more incense, or sigh for a few more fat offerings, let them say so plainly, instead of expressing their wishes by means of thunder, clouds, crows, bronze statues, and two-headed children. Moreover, you must admit, Lucius, theirs is a far too one-sided part when they presage the evils threatening us, since, in the natural course of things, not a day goes by but what brings some individual or public misfortune."

Gallio exhibited distress at the sorrows of Cassius.

"Claudius," he remarked, "Claudius, although he is always dozing, has deeply felt this great peril. He has complained to the Senate of the contempt into which ancient usages have been suffered to fall. Alarmed at the progress of foreign superstitions, the Senate has, on his recommendation, re-established haruspices. But it is not sufficient that the observance of the ceremonial rites of worship should be restored; rather is it necessary once more to instil into men's hearts their primitive purity. The souls of virtuous men constitute the proper shrine of the gods in this world. Give a home within your hearts to past virtues once more, simplicity, good faith, love of the public welfare, and the gods will immediately re-enter them. You shall then yourselves be temples and altars."

He spoke, and, taking leave of his friends, entered his litter, which, for some little time past, had been awaiting him near a clump of myrtle-bushes to convey him to the tribunal.

His friends had risen from their seats, and leaving the grounds, followed leisurely behind him under a double portico, so disposed as to afford shadow at all hours of the day, and leading from the walls of the villa to the basilica where the proconsul dispensed justice.

By the way, Lucius Cassius expressed to Mela his regret at the oblivion into which the ancient methods of discipline had fallen.

Marcus Lollius, placing a hand on the shoulder of Apollodorus, said:

"It seems to me that neither our gentle Gallio nor Mela, nor even Cassius, have stated their reasons for their deep hatred of the Jews. I think I know, and I am going to tell you, most dear Apollodorus. The Romans who offer up to the gods a white sow ornamented with white bands, execrate the Jews who refuse to partake of pork. It is not in vain that the fates sent to the pious Æneas a white female boar as a presage. Had the gods not studded with oaks the wild realms of Evander and Turnus, Rome would not be to-day the mistress of the world. The acorns of Latium fattened the swine whose flesh has alone appeased the insatiable hunger of the magnanimous descendants of Remus.

Our Italians, whose bodies are built on boars and pigs, feel offended at the proud abstinence of the Jews, who persist in casting aside as unclean vituals the fat sounders, beloved of old Cato, which furnish food to the masters of the Universe."

Thus discoursing pleasantly, and enjoying the kindly shade, the four friends reached the furthermost end of the portico, when of a sudden the Forum appeared before them in a glitter of light.

At that early hour, it was all astir with the coming and going of noisy crowds. In the centre of the square stood a bronze Minerva on a pedestal on which were sculptured the Muses, and to the right and to the left stood a Mercury and a bronze Apollo, the work of Hermogenes of Cythera. A Neptune with a green beard arose from the centre of a basin. At the feet of the god, a dolphin vomited forth water.

The Forum was surrounded in all directions by monuments, the high columns and the arches of which revealed the Roman style of architecture. Facing the portico by way of which Mela and his friends had come, the Propylæ, surmounted by two gilded chariots, formed the boundary of the public square, and led, by way of marble steps, to the broad and straight road of the harbour of Lechæum. On either side of these heroic gates rose in kingly fashion the painted pediments of the sanctuaries, the Pantheon, and the temple of Artemis of

Ephesus. The temple of Octavia, the sister of
Augustus, dominated the Forum, and looked upon
the sea.

Between it and the basilica ran an insignificant
little street. The building rose over two stories of
arcades supported by pillars flanked with Doric
half-columns forming a square. The Roman style,
which stamped its character upon all the other
buildings of the city, was patent. There remained
of the pristine Corinth nothing but the calcined
ruins of an old temple.

The lower arcades of the basilica were open and
served as shops to sellers of fruit, vegetables, oil,
wine and fried foods, to bird-fanciers, jewellers,
booksellers, and barbers. Money-changers sat at
little tables laden with gold and silver coins. From
the gloomy hollow of these stalls emerged shouts,
laughter, hailings, the noise of disputes, and pungent odours. On the marble steps, wherever their
slabs were tinted blue by the shade, loafers shook
dice or tossed knuckle-bones, suitors paced to and
fro with anxious mien, sailors gravely looked for
the pleasures upon which they should squander their
wages, while quidnuncs read news from Rome
written for them by frivolous Greeks. Blended
with this crowd of Corinthians and foreigners,
numerous blind beggars persistently obtruded themselves, as well as callow and rouged youths, match-
sellers and crippled sailors from whose necks de-

pended a picture of the wreck of their ships. Doves flew in flocks from the roof of the basilica down to the large open spaces on which the sun shone, and picked up grain between the cracks of the heated flagstones.

A girl of twelve, dark and velvety as a pansy of Xanthus, placed on the ground her little brother, as yet unable to walk, put beside him a chipped bowl filled with porridge and a wooden spoon, saying to him:

"Eat, Comatas, eat and keep quiet, or that red horse will have you."

Then, holding an obolus in her hand, she ran towards the fish-dealer, whose wrinkled face and naked breast, the colour of saffron, appeared amid baskets lined with seaweed.

While she was thus engaged, a dove hovering about the little Comatas got its talons entangled in the child's locks. The boy began to cry, and to call his sister to his help, screaming in a voice choked with sobs:

"Joessa! Joessa!"

But Joessa heard him not. She was rummaging in the old man's baskets, amid the fish and the shell-fish, for something that would improve the taste of her stale bread. Naturally she did not pick out a peacock-fish or a smaris, whose flesh is most delicate, but which cost money. She brought away in the hollow of her gown, which she had tucked up, three handfuls of sea-urchins and sticklebacks.

Meanwhile little Comatas, his mouth wide open, and drinking his own tears, was still bawling:

"Joessa! Joessa!"

Unlike Jove's eagle, the bird of Venus did not carry off little Comatas into the glorious skies. It left him on the earth, taking with it in its flight, between its pink talons, three golden hairs from his matted locks.

The child, with cheeks glistening with tears and begrimed with dust, clenching his wooden spoon in his tiny fists, was sobbing beside his overturned bowl.

Annæus Mela, followed by his three friends, had reached the top of the basilica's steps. Alike heedless of the noise and stir of the idle multitude, he was imparting information to Cassius in regard to the future renovation of the universe.

"On a day determined by the gods," he said, "the things existing to-day, whose order and disposition claim our attention, will be destroyed. Stars will clash with stars, all matters composing the earth, the air, and the waters will be consumed in one conflagration. Human souls, imperceptible *débris* amid the universal destruction, will be resolved anew into their primitive elements. An entirely new world . . ."

As he uttered the words, Annæus Mela stumbled

against a sleeper stretched out in the shade. It was an old man who had artistically gathered about his dust-covered body the ragged remnants of his cloak. His wallet, his sandals, and his stick lay beside him.

The proconsul's brother, ever courteous and kindly, even to men of the lowliest class, was about to apologise, but the recumbent individual did not allow him time to do so.

"Try and see where you put your feet, you brute," he exclaimed, "and give alms to the philosopher Posocharis."

"I perceive a wallet and a stick," smilingly replied the Roman, "but so far I do not see any philosopher."

Just as he was about to toss a piece of silver to Posocharis, Apollodorus stayed his hand, saying:

"Do not give him anything, Annæus. It is not a philosopher; nay, not even a man."

"But I am one," replied Mela, "if I give him money, and he is a man if he takes this coin. For, alone among all animals, man does both these things. And can you not see that for the sake of a small coin I satisfy myself that I am a better man than he? Your master teaches that he who gives is better than he who receives."

Posocharis took the coin. Then he hurled coarse invectives at Annæus Mela and his companions, stigmatising them as arrogant and as debauchees, and referring them to the jugglers and harlots who walked past them with undulating hips. Then, baring to the navel his hairy body, and drawing over his face his tattered cloak, he once more stretched himself out at full length on the pavement.

"Would it not interest you," asked Lollius of his companions, "to hear those Jews expound their dispute in the prætorium?"

They replied that they entertained no such curiosity, preferring to stroll under the portico, while waiting for the proconsul, who would doubtless not be long in coming out.

"I am with you, my friends," said Lollius. "We shall not miss anything very interesting."

"Moreover," he went on to say, "the Jews who have come from Cenchreæ to accompany the suitors are not all in the basilica. Here comes one who is recognisable by his beaked nose and his forked beard. He is in as fine a state of frenzy as Pythia herself."

Lollius was pointing with both look and finger at a lean stranger, poorly clad, who was vociferating under the portico, in the midst of a railing mob.

"Men of Corinth, you place a vain trust in your wisdom, which is naught but madness. You follow blindly the precepts of your philosophers who teach you death, and not life. You do not observe the natural law, and in order to punish you, God has delivered you unto unnatural vices. . . ."

A sailor, who had just joined the group of spectators, recognized the man, for, with a shrug of the shoulders, he muttered:

"Why, 'tis Stephanas, the Jew of Cenchreæ, who brings once more some extraordinary piece of news from his trip to the skies, into which he ascended, if we are to credit him."

And Stephanas was teaching the people.

"The Christian is not bound by law and concupiscence. He is exempt from damnation through the mercy of God, who sent his only son to assume a sinful body, in order to destroy sin. But ye shall only be delivered if, breaking with the flesh, you live according to the spirit.

"The Jews observe the laws, and believe that they are saved by their works. But it is their faith which saves them, and not their works. Of what use is it to them to be circumcised in fact, if their heart is uncircumcised?

"Men of Corinth, glory in the faith, and ye shall be incorporated into the family of Abraham."

The mob was beginning to laugh and jeer at these obscure utterances. Still the Jew continued prophesying in hollow tones. He was announcing a great manifestation of wrath and the all-destroying fire which was to consume the earth.

"And these things shall come to pass in my lifetime," he cried, "and I shall witness them with mine own eyes. The hour has come for us to

awaken from our sleep. The night has passed, and
the day is dawning. The Saints will rejoice in
Heaven, and those who have not believed in Jesus
crucified shall perish."

Then, promising the resurrection of the body, he
invoked Anastasis, amid the jeers of the hilarious
crowd.

Just then, a leather-lunged man, Milo the baker,
a member of the Corinthian Senate, who for some
time past had been listening to the Jew with impatience, came up to him, took him by the arm, and
shaking him roughly said:

"Cease, you wretch, spouting idle words. All
this is children's fables and nonsense fit to capture a
woman's mind. How canst thou, on the strength
of thy dreams, indulge in such foolery, casting aside
all that is beautiful, and taking pleasure in what is
evil only, without even deriving any advantage from
thy hatred? Renounce your strange phantasies,
your perverse designs, your gloomy forebodings,
lest a god abandon you to the crows, to punish you
for your imprecations against this city and the
Empire."

The citizens applauded Milo's speech.

"He speaks truly," they shouted. "Those
Syrians have but one design: they seek to weaken
our fatherland. They are the enemies of Cæsar."

A number of them abstracted from the fruiterers'
stalls gourds and locust-beans, others picked up

oyster-shells, and flung them at the apostle, who was still vaticinating.

Thrown down the steps of the portico, he wended his way through the Forum, shouting, amid a storm of hooting, insults, and blows, pelted with dirt, bleeding, and half naked:

"My Master has said it, we are the sweepings of the world."

And he exulted in his joy.

The children pursued him on the Cenchreæ road, yelling.

"Anastasis! Anastasis!"

Posocharis was not sleeping. Hardly had the friends of the proconsul gone away, when he raised himself upon his elbow. Seated on a step, a short distance from him, the swarthy Joessa was crunching between her teeth the shell of a sea-urchin. The cynic hailed her and showed her the glittering piece of silver he had just received. Then, having readjusted his rags and tatters, he rose, slipped his feet into his sandals, picked up his stick and wallet, and went down the steps. Joessa went up to him, relieved him of his wallet full of holes, which she gravely placed on her shoulder, as if to carry it as an offering to the august Cypris, and followed the old man.

Apollodorus saw them taking the Cenchreæ road with the object of reaching the cemetery of the slaves, and the place of execution conspicuous from afar by the swarms of crows which hovered over the crosses. The philosopher and the young girl knew there a clump of arbutus always deserted, and favourable to dalliance with Eros.

At the sight of this, Apollodorus, pulling Mela by the flap of his toga, remarked:

"Just look. No sooner has that cur received your alms than he decoys a child, in order to mate with her."

"Which goes to prove," answered Mela, "that I gave money to the kind of man who knows full well what to do with it."

Meanwhile, the brat Comatas, squatting on the heated flagstone and sucking his thumbs, was laughing at the sight of a pebble glistening in the sun.

"Besides," resumed Mela, "you must admit, Apollodorus, that the way in which Posocharis makes love is not a bit philosophical. The dog is assuredly wiser than our young debauchees of the Palatine, who love amid perfumes, tears, and laughter, with languor or with passion. . . ."

As he spoke, a hoarse clamour arose in the prætorium, deafening to the ears of the Greek and the three Romans.

"By Pollux!" exclaimed Lollius, "the suitors whose case our friend Gallio is trying are shouting like dockers, and it seems to me that together with their growls a stench of sweat and onions reaches us."

"Nothing is more true," quoth Apollodorus. "But, were Posocharis a philosopher instead of the dog he is, far from sacrificing to the Venus of the cross-roads, he would flee from the whole breed of women, and attach himself solely to some youth, whose eternal comeliness he would contemplate merely as the expression of an inner beauty more noble and more precious."

"Love," resumed Mela, "is an abject passion. It disturbs the reason, destroys noble impulses, and diverts the most elevated ideas to the vilest cares. It has no place in a sensible mind. As the poet Euripides teaches us . . ."

Mela did not finish his sentence. Preceded by lictors, who pushed the crowd aside, the proconsul came out of the basilica, and went up to his friends.

"I have not been away from you long," he said. "The case which I was summoned to try was as meagre as could be, and ridiculous in the extreme. On entering the prætorium, I found it invaded by a motley crowd of Jews who, in their sordid shops along the wharves of the harbour of Cenchreæ, sell carpets, stuffs, and petty articles of silver and gold jewellery to the sailors. The atmosphere was filled with their shrill yelping, and with a pungent odour of goat. It was with difficulty that I could grasp the meaning of their words, and it cost me an effort to understand that one of those Jews, Sosthenes by name, who styled himself the chief of the synagogue, was charging with impiety another Jew, the latter, repulsively ugly, bandy-legged, and blear-eyed, and named Paul or Saul, a native of Tarsus, who has for some time past been exercising in Corinth his trade of weaver, and has gone into partnership with certain Jews expelled from Rome, for the weaving of tent-cloths and Cilician garments in goat-hair. They all spoke at once, and in very bad Greek. I made out, however, that this Sosthenes imputed as a crime to this Paul that he had entered the house wherein the Jews of Corinth are in the habit of meeting every Saturday, and had spoken with the object of seducing his co-religionists, and of persuading them to worship their god in a fashion contrary to their law. I had heard enough. So having, not without difficulty, silenced them, I informed them that had they come to me to complain of some matter of wrong or of some deed of violence wherefrom they might have suffered injury, I should have listened to them with patience, and with all the necessary attention; but, since their case turned simply upon a question of words, and a disagreement in regard to their law, it concerned me not, and that I could not be judge of such matters. I thereupon dismissed them with these words: 'Settle your quarrels among yourselves, as best you see fit.' "

"What did they say to that?" asked Cassius.

"Did they submit with good grace to so wise a decision?"

"It is not in the nature of brutes," replied the proconsul, "to relish wisdom. Those fellows greeted my decision with harsh murmurings of which, as you may well imagine, I took no notice. I left them shouting and struggling at the foot of the tribunal. From what I could see, most of the blows fell to the plaintiff. He will be left for dead, if my lictors do not interfere. These Jews from the harbour are great ignoramuses, and like most ignorant people, not enjoying the faculty of supporting with arguments the truth of what they believe, they know no other argument than kicks and fisticuffs.

"The friends of that little deformed and bleareyed Jew named Paul seem to be particularly clever at that kind of controversy. Ye gods! How they got the better of the chief of the synagogue, raining blows on him, and trampling him under their feet! But I do not doubt that had the friends of Sosthenes been the stronger of the two parties, they would have treated Paul as the friends of Paul treated Sosthenes."

Mela congratulated the proconsul.

"You were right, brother mine, in sending those wretched litigants about their business."

"Could I do otherwise?" replied Gallio. "How

could I have decided between that Sosthenes and
that Paul who are the one as stupid and as rabid as
the other? . . . If I treat them with contempt, do
not, my friends, think that is because they are poor
and humble, because Sosthenes reeks of salted fish,
or for the reason that Paul's fingers have become
worn in weaving carpets and tent-cloth. No,
Philemon and Baucis were poor, yet worthy of the
highest honours. The gods did not disdain being
entertained at their frugal board. Wisdom raises
a slave above his master. Nay, a virtuous slave is
superior to the gods. If he is their equal in wisdom,
he surpasses them in the beauty of the accomplishment. Those Jews are to be despised simply because they are boorish, and that no image of the
divinity is reflected in them."

A smile overspread the countenance of Marcus
Lollius at these words.

"Truly, the gods," he said, "would hardly frequent the Syrians who infest the harbours, amid the
sellers of fruit and the strumpets."

"The Barbarians themselves," resumed the proconsul, "possess some knowledge of the gods. Not
to mention the Egyptians, who, in the olden days,
were men filled with piety, there is not in wealthy
Asia a nation which has not worshipped Diana.
Vulcan, Juno, or the mother of the Æneædes.
They give these divinities strange names, confused
forms, and sometimes offer up to them human

sacrifices, but they recognise their power. Alone
are the Jews ignorant of the providence of the gods.
I know not whether that Paul, whom the Syrians
also call Saul, is as superstitious as the others, and as
obstinate in his errors. I know not what obscure
ideas he conceives of the immortal gods, and to tell
the truth, I am not concerned to know it. What is
there to be learned of those who know nothing! It
amounts, to put it plainly, to educating oneself in
ignorance. I gathered from some of his confused
expressions in my presence and in reply to his accuser, that he joins issue with the priests of his
nation, that he repudiates the religion of the Jews,
and that he worships Orpheus under an assumed
name which has escaped me. What makes me
suppose this, is that he speaks with respect of a god,
or rather of a hero, who is supposed to have
descended into Hades, and to have reascended into
the heavens, after having wandered among the
pallid shades of the dead. He may perhaps have
set himself to worship some subterranean Mercury.
I should, however, feel more inclined to believe that
he worships Adonis, for I think I heard him say
that, following in the steps of the women of Byblos,
he wept over the sufferings and the death of a god.

"These youthful gods, who die and come to life
again, abound on Asiatic soil. The Syrian courte-
sans have brought several of them to Rome, and
these celestial youths please, more than is proper,

our respectable women. Our matrons do not blush
to celebrate their mysterious rites in private. My
Julia, so prudent and so self-contained, has re-
peatedly asked me how much should be believed of
them. 'What kind of a god,' have I answered her
with indignation, 'what can be the god who takes
delight in the stealthy homage of a married dame?
A woman should know no other friends than those
of her husband. And do not the gods stand first in
order among our friends?' "

"Does not this man of Tarsus," inquired the
philosopher Apollodorus, "pay reverence rather to
Typhon, whom the Egyptians call Sethon? It is
said that a god with an ass's head is shown honour
by a certain Jewish sect. This god can be no other
than Typhon, and I should not be surprised if the
weavers of Cenchreæ held a secret intercourse with
the Immortal, who, according to our gentle Marcus,
committed so disgusting an outrage on the old
woman who sold cakes."

"I know not," resumed Gallio. "They do indeed say that a number of Syrians meet to celebrate
in secret the worship of a god with a donkey's head.
It may be that Paul is one of them. But what
matters the Adonis, the Mercury, the Orpheus, or
the Typhon of that Jew? He will never reign over
any but the female fortune-tellers, the usurers, and
the sordid traders who spoil the sailors in seaports.

At the very utmost will he be able to win over, in the suburbs of the big cities, a few handfuls of slaves."

"Oho! Oho!" exclaimed Marcus Lollius in an outburst of laughter, "can you see that hideous Paul founding a religion of slaves? By Castor, it would indeed be a miraculous novelty! Should perchance the god of the slaves (may Jove avert the omen!) climb up into Olympus and expel therefrom the gods of the empire, what would he do in turn? In what way would he exercise his power over the astonished world? I should enjoy seeing him at work. He would no doubt keep up the Saturnalia during the entire course of the year. He would open to gladiators the road to the highest honours, establish the prostitutes of the Suburra in the temple of Vesta, and perhaps make of some wretched straggling village in Syria the capital of the world."

Lollius might have followed up his jest for some time had Gallio not interrupted him.

"Marcus," he said, "do not entertain the hope of witnessing these marvellous novelties. Although men are capable of stupendous acts of folly, it is not a little Jew weaver who could seduce them with his bad Greek and his tales about a Syrian Orpheus. The slaves' god could but foment uprisings and servile wars, which would be promptly put down in blood, and he would soon perish himself, together with his worshippers, in an amphitheatre, under the teeth of wild beasts, to the plaudits of the Roman people.

"Enough of Paul and Sosthenes. Their mind would not be of any help to us in the quest we were engaged upon ere they so untowardly interrupted us. We were seeking to know the future the gods have in store for us, not for you, dear friends, or for me in particular (for we are prepared to endure all that is to be), but for the fatherland and for the human race which we love and towards which we feel kindly. It is not that Jew weaver, with his inflamed eyelids, who could tell us, whatever Marcus may think, the name of the god who is to dethrone Jupiter."

Gallio broke off his speech to dismiss the lictors, who stood motionless in line before him, shouldering their fasces.

"We require neither the rods nor the axes," he remarked with a smile. "Speech is our only weapon. May the day come when the universe shall know no others. If you are not tired, my friends, let us walk towards the Pirene fountain. We shall find midway an old fig-tree under which, so it is related, the betrayed Medea meditated her cruel revenge. The Corinthians hold the tree in reverence, in memory of that jealous queen, and suspend votive tablets from its branches, for Medea never brought them but good. It has cleft the earth with its branches, which have thrown out roots, and it is still crowned with a luxuriant foliage. Seated in its shade, we can while away time with conversation till our bath-hour."

The children, weary of pursuing Stephanas, were playing at knuckle-bones by the roadside. The apostle was striding along rapidly, when he came across, near the place of execution, a band of Jews, who had come up from Cenchreæ to ascertain the judgment rendered by the proconsul in regard to the synagogue. They were friends of Sosthenes, and were greatly irritated against the Jew of Tarsus and his adherents because they sought to change the law. Noticing the man, who was wiping with his sleeve his eyes blinded with blood, they thought they recognised him, and one of them, pulling him by the beard, asked if he were not Stephanas, the companion of Paul.

Proudly he answered:

"Behold him!"

He was quickly thrown to the ground, and trampled under foot. The Jews were picking up stones and shouting:

"He is a blasphemer! Stone him!"

A couple of the most zealous tore up the milestone sunk by the Romans, and were endeavouring to heave it at him. The stones fell with a dull thud on the skinny bones of the apostle, who yelled:

"Oh the delight of these wounds! Oh the joy

of these sufferings! Oh the refreshment of this torture! I behold Jesus."

A few steps farther off, under an arbutus, and to the murmurings of a spring, old Posocharis was pressing in his arms the smooth flanks of Joessa. Annoyed at the disturbance, he growled with a choking voice, with head buried in the hair of the young girl:

"Begone, you low brutes, and do not trouble a philosopher's pastime."

After a few minutes, a centurion who was passing along the now deserted road, raised Stephanas from the ground, made him swallow a mouthful of wine, and gave him linen wherewith to bandage his wounds.

While this was going on, Gallio, sitting with his friends under Medea's tree, was saying:

"If you wish to know the successor of the master of gods and men, meditate the words of the poet:

" 'Jove's spouse shall bring forth a son more powerful than his father.'

"This line designates, not the august Juno, but the most illustrious among the noble women with whom consorted the Olympian who so often changed his form and his loves. It seems to me assured that the government of the universe is to fall to the lot of Hercules. This opinion has long

since taken root in my mind, by reasons derived not
only from the poets, but from philosophers and men
of science. I have, so to speak, greeted by antic-
ipation the accession of the son of Alcmene, in the
climax of my tragedy of *Hercules on Œta*, ending
with the following words:

"'Hail, great conqueror of monsters, and pacifier of the
world; be propitious unto us! Cast thy gaze upon the
earth, and if some monster of a new kind strike terror into
mankind, destroy it with a thunderbolt. Better than thy
father wilt thou know how to hurl thunder.'

"I augur favourably of the coming reign of
Hercules. During his life upon earth, he displayed
a spirit patient and inclined to elevated thoughts.
When the time comes for thunder to arm his band,
he will not suffer a new Caius to govern the Empire
with impunity. Virtue, ancient simplicity, courage,
innocence, and peace will reign with him. Thus do
I prophesy."

And Gallio, having risen, took leave of his friends
with these words:

"Fare ye well, and love me."

III

S Nicole Langelier came to the end of his reading, the birds heralded by Giacomo Boni filled the deserted Forum with their friendly cries.

The sky was spreading over the Roman ruins the ash-tinted veil of evening; the young laurel-bushes planted along the Via Sacra lifted up into the diaphanous atmosphere their branches black as antique bronzes, while the flanks of the Palatine were clothed in azure.

"Langelier," spoke M. Goubin, who was not easily deceived, "you did not invent that story. The suit brought by Sosthenes against St. Paul before Gallio, proconsul of Achaia, is to be found in the *Acts of the Apostles.*"

Nicole Langelier readily admitted the fact.

"The story is told," he said, "in chapter xviii., and occupies verses 12 to 17 inclusively, which I am able to read to you, for I copied them on to a sheet of my manuscript."

Whereupon he read:

" '12. And when Gallio was the deputy of Achaia, the Jews made insurrection with one accord against Paul, and brought him to the judgment seat,

" '13. Saying, This *fellow* persuadeth men to worship God contrary to the law.

" '14. And when Paul was now about to open *his* mouth, Gallio said unto the Jews, If it were a matter of wrong or wicked lewdness, O *ye* Jews, reason would that I should bear with you:

" '15. But if it be a question of words and names, and *of* your law, look ye *to it*; for I will be no judge of such *matters.*

" '16. And he drove them from the judgment seat.

" '17. Then all the Greeks took Sosthenes, the chief ruler of the synagogue, and beat him before the judgment seat. And Gallio cared for none of those things.'

"I have not invented anything," added Langelier. "Little is known of Annæus Mela, and of Gallio, his brother. It is, however, certain that they were numbered among the most intelligent men of their day. When Achaia, a senatorial province under Augustus, an imperial one under Tiberius, was restored to the Senate by Claudius, Gallio was sent thither as proconsul. He was doubtless indebted for the post to the influence of his brother Seneca; it is possible, however, that he was selected for his knowledge of Greek literature, and as a man agreeable to the Athenian professors, whose intellects the Romans admired. He was highly educated. He had written a book on physiological subjects, and, it is believed, some few tragedies. His works are all lost, unless something from his pen is to be met with in the collection of tragic recitations attributed

without sufficient reasons to his brother the philosopher. I have assumed that he was a Stoic, and
that he held in many respects the same opinions as
his illustrious brother. But, while placing in his
mouth words of virtue and rectitude, I have guarded
against attributing any settled doctrine to him.
The Romans of those days blended the ideas of
Epicurus with those of Zenon. I was not incurring
any great risk of being mistaken, when investing
Gallio with this eclecticism. I have represented
him as a kindly man. He was that, assuredly.
Seneca has said of him that no one loved him in a
lukewarm fashion. His gentleness was universal.
He aspired to honours.

"Quite the contrary, his brother Annæus Mela
held aloof from them. We have on that point the
testimony of Seneca the philosopher, as well as that
of Tacitus. When Helvia, the mother of the three
Senecas, lost her husband, the most famed of her
sons indited a small philosophical treatise for her.
In a certain part of this work, he exhorts her to
consider, in order to reconcile her to life, that there
remain unto her sons like Gallio and Mela, differing
as to character, but equally worthy of her affection.

" 'Cast thine eyes upon my brothers,' he says, or
words to that effect. 'Both shall, by the diversity
of their virtues, charm thy weary moments. Gallio
has attained honours through his talents. Mela
has despised them in his wisdom. Derive enjoy-

ment from the regard in which the one is held, from the calm of the other, and from the love of both. I know the inner sentiments of my brothers. Gallio seeks in dignities an ornament for thyself. Mela embraces a gentle and peaceful life in order to devote himself to thee.'

"A child during the principality of Nero, Tacitus did not know the Senecas. He merely collected what was currently said about them in his day. He states that if Mela held aloof from honours, it was through a refinement of ambition, and, a simple Roman knight, to rival the influence of the consular officers. After having administered in person the vast estates he possessed in Boetica, Mela came to Rome, and had himself appointed administrator of Nero's estate. The conclusion was drawn therefrom that he was shrewd in matters of business, and he was even suspected of not being as disinterested as he wished to appear. That may be. The Senecas, while parading their contempt for riches, were possessed of great wealth, and it is very hard to believe the tutor of Nero when, amid the luxury of his furniture and his gardens, he represents himself as faithful to his beloved poverty. Still, the three sons of Helvia were not ordinary souls. Mela had of Atilla, his wife, a son, Lucan the poet. It would seem that Lucan's talent reflected great lustre on his father's name. Letters were then held in high honour, and eloquence and poetry ranked above all things.

"Seneca, Mela, Lucan, and Gallio perished with the accomplices of Piso. Seneca the philosopher was already an aged man. Tacitus, who had not been a witness of his death, has portrayed the scene for us. We know how Nero's tutor opened his veins while in his bath, and how his young wife Paulina protested that she would die with him, and by a similar death. By Nero's order, Paulina's wrists, which had been opened at the veins, were bandaged. She lived, preserving thereafter a deathly pallor. Tacitus records that young Lucan, whilst under torture, denounced his mother. Even if there were confirmation of this infamous deed, the blame for it should be laid to the tortures he underwent. But there is certainly one reason for not believing it. If indeed pain extorted from Lucan the names of several of the conspirators, he did not pronounce that of Atilla, since Atilla was not molested at a time when every information was blindly credited.

"After the death of Lucan, Mela, with too great a haste and diligence, seized on the inheritance of his son. A friend of the young poet, who doubtless coveted the inheritance, became the accuser of Mela. It was alleged that the father had been initiated into the secret of the conspiracy, and a forged letter of

Lucan was brought forth. Nero, after having read it, ordered it to be shown to Mela. Following the example set by his brother and so many of Nero's victims, Mela caused his veins to be opened, after having bequeathed a large sum of money to the freedmen of Cæsar, in order to secure the remainder of his fortunes to the unhappy Atilla. Gallio did not survive his two brothers; he took his own life.

"Such was the tragic end of these charming and cultured men. I have made two of them, Gallio and Mela, speak in Corinth. Mela was a great traveller. His son Lucan, while yet a child, was on a visit to Athens, at the time Gallio was proconsul of Achaia. There is therefore some show of reason for saying that Mela was then with his brother in Corinth. I have supposed that two young Romans of illustrious birth, and a philosopher of the Areopagus, accompanied the proconsul. In so doing, I have not taken too great a liberty, since the intendants, the procurators, the proprætors, and the proconsuls whom the Emperor and the Senate respectively sent to govern the provinces, always had about themselves the sons of great families, who came to instruct themselves in the management of public affairs under their guidance, and that of men of keen intellect like my Apollodorus, more frequently freedmen acting as their secretaries. Lastly, I conceived the idea that at the moment St. Paul was

being brought before a Roman tribunal, the proconsul and his friends were conversing freely about the
most varied subjects, art, philosophy, religion, and
politics, and that there pierced the various topics
absorbing their interest a deep anxiety as to the future. There is indeed some likelihood that on that
very day, just as well as on any other, they may have
sought to discover the future destiny of Rome and
the world. Gallio and Mela stood among the most
elevated and open intellects of the day. Minds of
such calibre are at all times inclined to delve into the
present and the past for the conditions of the future.
I have noticed in the most learned and well-
informed men whom I have known, to name but
Renan and Berthelot, a pronounced tendency to in-
terject at haphazard into a conversation outlines of
rational utopias and scientific forecasts."

"Here then we have," said Joséphin Leclerc,
"one of the best educated men of his day, a man
versed in philosophic speculation, trained in the conduct of public affairs, and who was of as open and
broad a mind as could be that of a Roman such as
Gallio, the brother of Seneca, the ornament and
light of his century. He is concerned about the future, he seeks to grasp the movement which is most
affecting the world, and he tries to fathom the destiny of the Empire and the gods. Just then, by a
unique stroke of fortune, he comes across St. Paul;
the future he is in quest of passes by him, and he

sees it not. What an example of the blindness which strikes, in the very presence of an unexpected revelation, the most enlightened minds and the keenest intellects!"

"I would have you observe, my dear friend," replied Nicole Langelier, "that it was not a very easy matter for Gallio to converse with St. Paul. It is not easy to conceive how they could possibly have exchanged ideas. St. Paul had trouble in expressing himself, and it was with great difficulty that he made himself intelligible to the folk who lived and thought like himself. He had never spoken word of mouth to any cultured man.

"He was nowise capable of indicating a train of thought and of following those of an interlocutor. He was ignorant of Greek science. Gallio, accustomed to the conversation of educated people, had long since trained his reason to debate. He knew not the maxims of the rabbis. What then could these two men have said to each other?

"Not that it was impossible for a Jew to converse with a Roman. The Herods enjoyed a mode of expression which was agreeable to Tiberius and Caligula. Flavius Josephus and Queen Berenice discoursed in terms pleasing to Titus, the destroyer of Jerusalem. We know that bejewelled Jews were at all times to be found in company of the antisemites. They were *meschoumets* (accursed unbelievers—anathema to Paul). Paul was a *nebi* (prophet). This fiery and haughty Syrian, disdainful of the worldly goods sought for by all men, thirsting after poverty, ambitious of insults and humiliations, rejoicing in suffering, was merely able to proclaim his sombre and inflamed visions, his hatred of life and of the beautiful, his absurd outbursts of anger, and his insane charity. Apart from this, he had nothing to say. In truth, I can discover one subject only on which he might have agreed with the proconsul of Achaia. 'Tis Nero.

"St. Paul, at that time, could hardly have heard any mention of the youthful son of Agrippina, but on learning that Nero was destined to Imperial power, he would immediately become a Neronian. He became so later on. He was still one at the time Nero poisoned Britannicus. Not that he was capable of approving of a brother's murder, but because he entertained a profound respect for all government. 'Let every soul be subject unto the higher powers,' he wrote to his churches. 'For rulers are not a terror to good works, but to the evil. Wilt thou then not be afraid of the power? Do that which is good, and thou shalt have praise of the same.' Gallio might perchance have found these maxims somewhat simple and commonplace, but he could not have disapproved of them as a whole. But if there is a subject which he would not have felt tempted to approach while speaking with a Jewish weaver, it is indeed the ruling of people and the authority of the Emperor. Once more, what could those two men well have said to each other?

"In our own day, when a European official in Africa, let us say the Governor-General of the Sudan for his Britannic Majesty, or our Governor of Algeria, comes across a fakeer or a marabout, their conversation is naturally confined within restricted limits. St. Paul was to a proconsul what a marabout is to our civil Governor of Algeria. A conversation between Gallio and St. Paul would have resembled only too much, I imagine, that held by General Desaix with his famous dervish. After the battle of the Pyramids, General Desaix, at the head of twelve hundred cavalry, pursued into Upper Egypt the Mamelukes of Murad Bey. On arriving at Girgeh, he heard that an old dervish, who had acquired among the Arabs a wide reputation for learning and sanctity, was living near that city. Desaix was endowed with both philosophy and humanity. Desirous of making the acquaintance of a man esteemed of his fellows, he caused the dervish to be summoned to headquarters, received him with honour, and entered into conversation with him through an interpreter.

" 'Venerable old man,' he said, 'the French have come to bring Egypt justice and liberty.'

" 'I knew they would come,' replied the dervish.

" 'How did you come to know it?'

" 'Through an eclipse of the sun.'

" 'How can an eclipse of the sun have informed you as to the movement of our armies?'

" 'Eclipses are brought about by the angel Gabriel, who places himself before the sun in order to announce to the faithful the misfortunes which threaten them.'

" 'Venerable old man, you are ignorant of the true cause of eclipses; I shall impart the knowledge of it to you.'

"Thereupon, taking a stump of pencil and a scrap of paper, he traced some figures:

" 'Let A be the sun, B, the moon, C, the earth,' and so forth . . .

"And when he had come to the end of his demonstration,

" 'Such,' he said, 'is the theory governing eclipses of the sun.'

"And as the dervish was mumbling a few words,

" 'What does he say?' asked the General of the interpreter.

" 'General, he says that it is the angel Gabriel who causes eclipses, by placing himself in front of the sun.'

" 'The fellow is simply naught but a fanatic!' exclaimed Desaix.

"Whereupon he drove the dervish out with well-administered kicks.

"I imagine that had a conversation been entered

into between St. Paul and Gallio, it would have ended somewhat as did the dialogue between the dervish and General Desaix."

"It must, however, be pointed out," said Joséphin Leclerc, joining issue, "that between the Apostle Paul and the dervish of General Desaix, there is at the very least this difference: the dervish did not impose his faith on Europe. And you will admit that his Britannic Majesty's honourable Governor of the Sudan has doubtless not come across the marabout who is to confer his name on the biggest church in London; you must likewise admit that our civil Governor of Algeria has never come face to face with the founder of a religion which the majority of the French nation will some day believe and profess. These functionaries have not seen the future arise before them under a human form. The proconsul of Achaia did."

"It was none the less impossible for Gallio," replied Langelier, "to carry on with St. Paul a steady conversation on some important subject regarding morals or philosophy. I am well aware, and you yourselves are not ignorant of the fact, that towards the fifth century of the Christian Era, it was believed that Seneca had known St. Paul in Rome, and had expressed admiration of the Apostle's doctrines. This fable owed its spread to the deplorable clouding of the human mind following so closely upon the age of Tacitus and of Trajan. In order

to obtain credence for it, certain forgerers, who at
that time swarmed in Christian ranks, fabricated a
correspondence which is mentioned respectfully by
St. Jerome and St. Augustine. If these letters are
those which have come unto us ascribed to Paul and
Seneca, it must be that those two Fathers did not
read them, or that they greatly lacked discernment.
It is the absurd work of a Christian utterly ignorant
of everything connected with Nero's time, and one
totally incapable of imitating Seneca's style. Is it
necessary to say that the great divines of the Middle
Ages firmly believed in the truth of the intercourse
between the two men and in the genuineness of the
letters? But the classical scholars of the Renaissance
had no difficulty in demonstrating the unlikelihood
and the falsity of these inventions. It matters little that Joseph de Maistre should have garnered by
the way this antiquated rubbish together with much
of the same kind. No one any longer heeds it, and
henceforth it is only in pretty novels written for
society by skilful and mystical authors that the
apostles of the primitive Church converse freely
with the philosophers and people of fashion of Imperial Rome and expound to the delight of Petro-
nius the novel beauties of Christianity. The words
of Gallio and his friends, which you have just heard,
are endowed with less charm and more truth."

"I do not deny it," replied Joséphin Leclerc, "and
I believe that the personages of the dialogue are

made to think and speak as they must actually have
thought and spoken, and that the ideas entertained
by them are those of their day. Therein, it seems
to me, lies the merit of the work, and therefore do I
reason about it just as if I were basing my arguments
on a historical text."

"You may safely do so," said Langelier. "I
have not embodied in it anything for which I have
not the authority of a reference."

"Very well then," resumed Joséphin Leclerc, "so
we have been listening to a Greek philosopher and
several Roman literati engaged in speculations as to
the future destinies of their fatherland, of humanity
and of the earth, and seeking to discover the name
of Jove's successor. The while they are absorbed in
this perplexing quest, the apostle of the new god
appears before them, and they treat him with contempt. I maintain that in so doing they plainly
show a lack of penetration, and lose through their
own fault a unique opportunity of becoming instructed concerning that which they felt so great a
desire to know."

"It seems self-evident to you, my good friend,"
replied Nicole Langelier, "that Gallio, had he known
how to set about it, would have gathered from St.
Paul the secret of the future. Such is perhaps the
first idea that springs to the mind, and it is one that
many have become imbued with. Renan, after having recorded, according to the *Acts*, this singular

interview between Gallio and St. Paul, is not averse from discovering evidence of a narrow and thoughtless mind in the contempt experienced by the proconsul for this Jew of Tarsus who appeared before his tribunal. He seizes the opportunity thus offered to lament the poor philosophy of the Romans. 'What a lack of foresight,' he exclaims, 'is sometimes exhibited by intellectual men! In later times, it was to be discovered that the squabble between those abject sectarians was the great event of the century.' Renan seems to believe that the proconsul of Achaia had merely to listen to that weaver in order to be there and then informed of the spiritual revolution in course of preparation throughout the universe, and to penetrate the secret of future humanity. And this is also no doubt what every one thinks at first sight. Nevertheless, ere settling the point, let us look more closely into the matter; let us examine what both men expected, and let us find out which of the two was, when all is said and done, the better prophet.

"In the first place, Gallio believed that the youthful Nero would be an emperor of philosophic mind, govern according to the maxims of the Portico, and be the delight of the human race. He was mistaken, and the reasons for his erroneous assumption are only too patent. His brother Seneca was the tutor of the son of Agrippina; his nephew, the boy Lucan, lived on terms of intimacy with the

young prince. Both his family and his personal
interests bound up the proconsul with the fortunes
of Nero. He believed that Nero would make an
excellent Emperor, for the wish was father to the
thought. His mistake arose rather from weakness
of character than from lack of intellect. Nero,
moreover, was then a youth full of gentleness, and
the early years of his principality were not to give
the lie to the hopes of the philosophers. Secondly,
Gallio believed that peace would reign over the
world after the chastisement of the Parthians. He
erred owing to a lack of knowledge of the actual
dimensions of the earth. He erroneously believed
that the *orbis Romanus* covered the whole of the
globe; that the inhabitable world ended at the burning or frozen strands, rivers, mountains, sands, and
deserts reached by the Roman eagles, and that the
Germani and Parthians peopled the confines of the
universe. We know how much weeping and blood
this error, shared in common by all Romans, cost
the Empire. Thirdly, Gallio, pinning his faith to
the oracles, believed in the eternity of Rome. He
was mistaken, if his prediction is to be taken in a
narrow and literal sense. But he was not so, if one
considers that Rome, the Rome of Cæsar and Trajan, has bequeathed us its customs and laws, and that
modern civilisation proceeds from Roman civilisation. It is in the august square where we now
stand that from the height of the rostral tribune and

in the Curia was debated the fate of the universe, and the form of constitution which to the present day governs the nations. Our science is based on Greek science transmitted to us by Rome. The reawakening of ancient thought in the fifteenth century in Italy, in the sixteenth century in France and Germany, was the cause of Europe being born anew in science and in reason. The proconsul of Achaia did not deceive himself: Rome is not defunct, since she lives in us. Let us, in the fourth place, examine Gallio's philosophical ideas. No doubt he was not equipped with a very sound natural philosophy, and he did not always interpret natural phenomena with sufficient precision. He applied himself to metaphysics as a Roman, *i. e.,* with a lack of acuteness. At heart, he valued philosophy merely because of its utility, and devoted himself mainly to moral questions. I have neither betrayed nor flattered him when placing his speeches on record. I have represented him as serious and mediocre, and a fairly good disciple of Cicero. You may have gathered that he reconciled, by dint of the poorest of reasoning, the doctrine of the Stoics to the national religion. One feels that whenever he indulges in speculation as to the nature of the gods, he is anxious to remain a good citizen and an honest official. But, after all, he thinks matters out, and reasons. The idea he conceives of the forces which govern the world is, in its principle, rational and scientific and, in this respect, it conforms to that which we have ourselves conceived of them. He does not reason as well as his friend the Greek Apollodorus. He does not argue any worse than the professors of our University who teach an independent philosophy and a Christian antimaterialism. By his open-mindedness and his strength of intelligence, he seems our contemporary. His thoughts turn naturally in the direction followed by the human mind at the present moment. Do not therefore let us say that he was unable to recognise the intellectual future of humanity.

"As to St. Paul, he announced the future; none doubt the fact. And yet he expected to see with his own eyes the world come to an end, and all things existing engulfed in flames. This conflagration of the universe, which Gallio and the Stoics foresaw in a future so remote that they none the less announced the eternity of the Empire, Paul believed to be quite close at hand, and was preparing for that great day. Herein he was mistaken, and you will admit that this misconception is in itself worse than all the united blunders of Gallio and his friends. Still more serious is it that Paul did not base this extraordinary belief on any observation or any reasoning whatever. He was ignorant of and despised science. He gave himself up to the lowest practices of thaumaturgy and glossology, and had no culture whatsoever.

"As a matter of fact, in regard to the future, as well as to the present and the past, there was nothing the proconsul could learn from the apostle, nothing but a mere name. Had he learnt that Paul was of Christ's religion, he would not have been any the better informed as to the future of Christianity, which was within a few years to disengage itself almost wholly from the ideas of Paul and of the first apostolic men. Thus it will be seen, if one does not pin one's opinion to liturgical texts, and to the strictly verbal interpretations of theologians, that St. Paul foresaw the future less accurately than Gallio, and one will be inclined to think that were the apostle to return to Rome nowadays, he would discover more cause for surprise than the proconsul.

"St. Paul, in modern Rome, would no more recognise himself on the column of Marcus Aurelius than he would recognise on the column of Trajan his old enemy Cephas. The dome of St. Peter's, the Stanze of the Vatican, the splendour of the churches, and the Papal pomp, all would offend his blinking eyes. In vain would he look for disciples in London, Paris, or Geneva. He would not understand either Catholics or Reformers who vie in quoting his real or supposed Epistles. Nor would he understand the minds freed from all dogma, who base their opinion on the two forces he hated and despised the most: science and reason. On dis-

covering that the Son of Man has not come, he
would rend his garments, and cover himself with
ashes."

Hippolyte Dufresne interrupted, saying:

"Whether in Paris or in Rome, there is no doubt
that St. Paul would be as an owl blinking in the
sun. He would be no more fit than a Bedouin of the
desert to communicate with cultured Europeans.
He would not know himself when at a bishop's, nor
would he obtain recognition from him. Were he to
alight at the house of a Swiss pastor fed upon his
writings, he would astound him with the primitive
crudity of his Christianity. All this is true. Bear
in mind, however, that he was a Semite, a foreigner
to Latin thought, to the genius of the Germani and
Saxons, to the races from which sprung those theologians who, by dint of erroneous conceptions, mis-
translations, and absurdities, discovered a meaning
in his counterfeit Epistles. You conceive him in a
world which was not his own, which can in no wise
become his, and this absurd conception at once gives
birth to an agglomeration of incongruous present-
ments. We picture to ourselves, to illustrate what I
say, this vagabond weaver sitting in a Cardinal's
coach, and we make merry over the appearance
presented by two human beings of so opposite a
character. If you persist in resurrecting St. Paul,
pray have the good taste to restore him to his race
and country, among the Semites of the East, who

have not greatly changed these twenty centuries, and for whom the Bible and the Talmud contain human science in its entirety. Drop him among the Jews of Damascus or of Jerusalem. Lead him to the Synagogue. There he will listen without astonishment to the teachings of his master, Gamaliel. He will enter into disputation with the rabbis, will weave goat-hair, live on dates and a little rice, observe the law faithfully, and of a sudden undertake to destroy it. He will in turn be persecutor and persecuted, executioner and martyr, all with equal keenness. The Jews of the Synagogue will proceed with his excommunication, by blowing into a ram's horn, and by spilling drop by drop the wax of black candles into a tub containing blood. He will endure without flinching this horrible ceremony, and will exercise, in the course of an arduous and continually menaced existence, the energy of a headstrong will. In such circumstances, he will probably be known to only a few ignorant and sordid Jews. But it will be Paul once more, and wholly Paul."

"That may be possible," said Joséphin Leclerc. "Yet you will grant me that St. Paul was one of the principal founders of Christianity, and that he might have imparted to Gallio valuable information concerning the great religious movement of which the proconsul was entirely ignorant."

"He who founds a religion," replied Langelier, "wots not what he does. I may say almost the same of those who found great human institutions, monastic orders, insurance companies, national guards, banks, trusts, trade unions, academies, schools of music and the drama, gymnastic societies, soup-kitchens, and lectures. Generally speaking, these establishments do not for any length of time carry out the intentions of their founders, and it sometimes happens that they become diametrically opposed to them. It is as much as one can do to trace after many long years a few vestiges of their founders' original intention. In the matter of religions, at any rate among nations whose existence is troublous and whose mind is fickle, they undergo so incessant and so complete a transformation, according to the feelings or interests of their faithful and their ministers, that in the course of a few years they preserve naught of the spirit which created them. Gods undergo more changes than men, for the reason that their form is less precise and that they endure longer. Some there are who improve as they grow older; others deteriorate with the years. It takes less than a century for a god to become unrecognisable. The god of the Christians has perhaps undergone a more complete transformation than any other. This is doubtless attributable to the fact that he has belonged in succession to the most varied civilisations and races, to the Latins, to the Greeks, to the Barbarians, and to all the nations sprung from the ruins of the Roman Empire. It is assuredly a far cry from the wooden Apollo of Dædalus to the classical Apollo Belvedere. Still greater a distance separates the youthful Christ of the Catacombs from the ascetic Christ of our cathedrals. This personage of the Christion mythology perplexes one by the number and variety of his metamorphoses. The flamboyant Christ of St. Paul is followed, as early as the second century, by the Christ of the Synoptic Gospels, a poor Jew, vaguely communistic, who becomes, with the Fourth Gospel, a sort of young Alexandrine, a milk-and-water disciple of the Gnostics. At a later period, if we only take into account the Roman Christs and tarry merely with the most famed of them, we have had the dominating Christ of Gregory VII., the bloodthirsty Christ of St. Dominic, the mob-leading Christ of Julius II., the atheistic and artistic Christ of Leo X., the indeterminate and insipid Christ of the Jesuits, Christ the protector of the factory, the defender of capital and the opponent of Socialism, who flourished under the pontificate of Leo XIII., and who still reigns. All those Christs, who have but the name in common, were not foreseen by Paul. In reality he knew no more than Gallio about the future god."

"You exaggerate," remarked M. Goubin, who disliked exaggeration in whatever form.

Giacomo Boni, who venerates the sacred books of all nations, here pointed out that Gallio and the

Roman philosophers and historians were to be blamed for not having a knowledge of the Jews' Sacred Scriptures.

"Had they been better informed," he said, "the Romans would not have harboured unjust prejudices against the religion of Israel; and, as your own Renan has said, a little goodwill and a better knowledge would perhaps have warded off fearful misunderstandings in regard to questions of interest to the whole of humanity. There lacked not educated Jews like Philo to explain the laws of Moses to the Romans, had the latter been more broad-minded and possessed a more correct presentiment of the future. The Romans experienced disgust and fear, when face to face with Asiatic thought. Even if they were right in fearing it, they were wrong in despising it. To despise a danger constitutes a great blunder. Gallio displayed want of foresight when stigmatising as criminal fancies and profanities of the vulgar the Syrian beliefs."

"How then could the Hellenist Jews have taught the Romans what they were themselves ignorant of?" inquired Langelier. "How could that honest Philo, so learned yet so shallow, have revealed to them the obscure, confused, and fecund thought of Israel, of which he knew nothing himself? What could he have imparted to Gallio concerning the faith of the Jews except literary absurdities? He would have explained to him that the doctrine of

Moses harmonises with the philosophy of Plato. Then, as always, cultured men had no idea of what was passing through the minds of the multitudes. The ignorant mob is for ever creating gods unknown to the literati.

"One of the strangest and most notable facts of history is the conquest of the world by the god of a Syrian tribe, and the victory of Jehovah over all the gods of Rome, Greece, Asia, and Egypt. Upon the whole, Jesus was simply a *nebi,* and the last of the prophets of Israel. Nothing is known about him. We are in the dark as to his life and death, for the Evangelists are in nowise biographers. As to the moral ideas grouped under his name, they originate in truth with the crowd of visionaries who prophesied in the days of the Herods.

"What is called the triumph of Christianity is more accurately the triumph of Judaism, and to Israel fell the singular privilege of giving a god to the world. It must be admitted that Jehovah deserved his sudden elevation in many respects. He was, when he attained to empire, the best of the gods. He had made a very bad beginning. Of him it may be said what historians say of Augustus, his heart softened with the years. At the time when the Israelites settled in the Promised Land, Jehovah was stupid, ferocious, ignorant, cruel, coarse, foul-mouthed, indeed the most silly and most cruel of gods. But, under the influence of the prophets,

there came about a complete transformation. He
ceased being conservative and formal, and became
converted to ideas of peace and to dreams of justice.
His people were wretched. He began to feel a
profound pity for all poor wretches. And although
he remained at heart very much a Jew and very
patriotic, he naturally became international when
becoming revolutionary. He constituted himself
the defender of the humble and oppressed. He
conceived one of those simple ideas which captivate
the world. He announced universal happiness, and
the coming of a beneficent Messiah whose reign
would be peace. His prophet Isaiah prompted him
as to this admirable theme with words delightfully
poetical and of unsurpassed softness:

" 'The mountain of the Lord's house shall be
established in the top of the mountains, and shall be
exalted above the hills; and all nations shall flow
unto it. And many people shall go and say, Come
ye and let us go up to the mountain of the Lord, to
the house of the God of Jacob; and he will teach us
of his ways, and we will walk in his paths: for out
of Zion shall go forth the law, and the word of the
Lord from Jerusalem. And he shall judge among
nations, and shall rebuke many people: and they
shall beat their swords into plowshares, and their
spears into pruning-hooks.

" 'The wolf also shall dwell with the lamb and
the leopard shall lie down with the kid; and the

calf and the young lion and the fatling together;
and a little child shall lead them.'

"In the Roman Empire, the god of the Jews set
himself to capture the working classes and the social
revolution. He addressed himself to the unfortunate. Now, in the days of Tiberius and Claudius,
there existed within the Empire infinitely more unhappy than happy ones. There were hordes of
slaves. One man alone owned as many as ten thousand. These slaves were for the most part sunk in
wretchedness. Neither Jupiter, nor Juno, nor the
Dioscuri troubled themselves about them. The
Latin gods did not pity their condition. They
were the gods of their masters. When came from
Judæa a god who hearkened to the complaints of
the humble, they worshipped him. So it is that the
religion of Israel became the religion of the Roman
world. This is what neither St. Paul nor Philo
could explain to the proconsul of Achaia, for they
themselves did not see it clearly. And this is what
Gallio could not realise. He felt, however, that
the reign of Jupiter was nearing its end, and he predicted the coming of a better god. From love of
the national antiquities, he went for this god to the
Græco-Latin Olympus, and selected him of the blood
of Jupiter, through aristocratic feeling. Thus it is
that he chose Hercules instead of Jehovah."

"For once," said Joséphin Leclerc, "you will admit that Gallio was mistaken."

"Less so than you think," replied Langelier with a smile. "Jehovah or Hercules, it mattered little. You may be sure of this: the son of Alcmene would not have governed the world otherwise than the father of Jesus. Olympian as he might be, he would have had to become the god of the slaves, and assume the religious spirit of the new times. The gods conform scrupulously to the sentiments of their worshippers: they have reasons for so doing. Pay attention to this. The spirit which favoured the accession in Rome of the god of Israel was not merely the spirit of the masses, but also that of the philosophers. At that time, they were nearly all Stoics, and believed in one god alone, one on whose behalf Plato had laboured and one unconnected by tie of family or friendship with the gods of human form of Greece and Rome. This god, through his infinity, resembled the god of the Jews. Seneca and Epictetus, who venerated him, would have been the first to have been surprised at the resemblance, had they been called upon to institute a comparison. Nevertheless, they had themselves greatly contributed towards rendering acceptable the austere monotheism of the Judæo-Christians. Doubtless a wide gulf separated Stoic haughtiness from Christian humility, but Seneca's morals, consequent upon his sadness and his contempt of nature, were paving the way for the Evangelical morals. The Stoics had joined issue with life and the beautiful; this rupture, attributed to Christianity, was initiated by the philosophers. A couple of centuries later, in the time of Constantine, both pagans and Christians will have, so to speak, the same morals and philosophy. The Emperor Julian, who restored to the Empire its old religion, which had been abolished by Constantine the Apostate, is justly regarded as an opponent of the Galilean. And, when perusing the petty treatises of Julian, one is struck with the number of ideas this enemy of the Christians held in common with them. He, like them, is a monotheist; with them, he believes in the merits of abstinence, fasting, and mortification of the flesh; with them, he despises carnal pleasures, and considers he will rise in favour with the gods by avoiding women; finally, he pushes Christian sentiment to the degree of rejoicing over his dirty beard and his black finger-nails. The Emperor Julian's morals were almost those of St. Gregory Nazianzen. There is nothing in this but what is natural and usual. The transformations undergone by morals and ideas are never sudden. The greatest changes in social life are wrought imperceptibly, and are only seen from afar. Christianity did not secure a foothold until such time as the condition of morals accommodated itself to it, and as Christianity itself had become adjusted to the condition of morals. It was unable to substitute itself for paganism until such time as paganism came to resemble it, and itself came to resemble paganism."

"Granted," said Joséphin Leclerc, "that neither St. Paul nor Gallio saw into the future. No one does. Has not one of your friends said: 'The future is concealed even from those who shape it'?"

"Our knowledge of what the future has in store," resumed Langelier, "is in proportion of our acquaintance with the present and the past. Science is prophetic. The more a science is accurate, the more can accurate prophesies be drawn from it. Mathematics, to which alone appertains entire accuracy, communicate a portion of their precision to the sciences proceeding from them. Thus it is that accurate predictions are made by means of mathematical astronomy and chemistry. One is able to calculate eclipses millions of years ahead, without fear of one's calculations being found erroneous, as long as the sun, the moon, and the earth shall preserve the same relations as to bulk and distance. It is even permitted to us to foresee that these relations will be modified in a far distant future. Indeed, it is prophesied, on the strength of the celestial mechanism, that the silver hornéd moon will not describe eternally the same circle round our globe, and that causes now in operation will, by dint of repetition, change its course. You may safely predict that the sun will become darkened, and will no longer appear except a shrunken globe over our icy seas, unless there should come to it in the interval some new alimentation, a thing quite within the possibilities, for the sun is capable of catching swarms of asteroids, just as a spider does flies. It is, however, safe to predict that it will become extinguished, and that the dislocated figures of the constellations will vanish star by star in the darkness of space. But what does the death of a star amount to? To the fading away of a spark. Let all the stars in the heavens die out just as the grasses of the field wither, what matters it to universal life, so long as the infinitely tiny elements composing them shall have retained within themselves the force which makes and unmakes worlds? It is safe to predict an even more complete end of the universe, the end of the atom, the dissociation of the last elements of matter, the times when protyle, when the amorphous fog will have reconquered its illimitable empire over the ruins of all things. And this will form but a breathing-spell in God's respiration. All will begin anew.

"The worlds will again be born to life. They will live again to die. Life and death will succeed each other for all eternity. All sorts of combinations will become facts in the infinity of space and time, and we shall find ourselves seated once more on the flank of the Forum in ruins. But as we shall not know that we are ourselves, it will not be us."

M. Goubin wiped his eye-glass.

"Such ideas are disheartening," he remarked.

"What then do you hope for, Monsieur Goubin," asked Nicole Langelier, "to gratify your wishes? Do you aspire to preserve of yourself and of the world an eternal consciousness? Why do you wish to remember for all time that you are Monsieur Goubin? I will not conceal it from you: the present universe, which is far from nearing its end, does not seem to possess the property of satisfying you in this respect. Do not place any more store in those which are to follow, for they will doubtless be of the same kind. Do not, however, abandon all hope. It is possible that after an indefinite successions of universes, you shall be born anew, Monsieur Goubin, with a recollection of your previous existences. Renan has said that it was a risk to be taken, and that at all events it would not be long in coming. The successions of universe will take place for us within less than a second. Time does not count for the dead."

"Are you cognisant," asked Hippolyte Defresne, of the astronomical dreams of Blanqui? The aged Blanqui, a prisoner in the Mont-Saint-Michel, could get but a glimpse of the sky through his stopped-up window, and had the stars for his only neighbours. This made of him an astronomer, and he based on the unity of matter and the laws ruling it a strange theory in regard to the identity of the worlds. I have read a sixty-page pamphlet of his wherein he sets forth that form and life are developed in exactly the same manner in a large number of worlds. According to him, a multitude of suns, all similar to our own, have, do, or will shed light upon planets in every respect similar to the planets of our own system. There is, was, and will be, *ad infinitum*, Venuses, Mars, Saturns, and Jupiters, quite the counterpart of our Saturn, Mars, and Venus, and worlds similar to our own. These worlds produce exactly what our world produces, and bear fruits, animals, and men resembling in all respects terrestrial plants, animals, and human beings. The evolution of life in them is the same as that on our globe. Consequently, thought the aged prisoner, there is, was and shall be throughout the infinite space myriads of Monts-Saint-Michel, each containing a Blanqui."

"We know but little of the worlds whose suns shine upon our nights," resumed Langelier. "We perceive, however, that subjected to the same mechanical and chemical laws, they differ from our own world and among themselves in extent and form, and that the substances burning in them are not distributed among all of them in the same proportions. These differences must produce an infinity of others which we do not suspect. A pebble is sufficient to change the fate of an Empire. Who knows? Perchance, Monsieur Goubin, many times

multiplied and disseminated through myriads of
worlds, has wiped, wipes, and shall eternally wipe
clean his eye-glass."

Joséphin Leclerc did not suffer his friends to ex-
patiate any further on astronomical dreams.

"I am," he said, "like Monsieur Goubin, of the
opinion that all this would be heartrending were it
not too far from us to affect us. What is of paramount interest for us, what we are curious to know
is the fate of those who will come immediately after
us in this world."

"There is no doubt," said Langelier, "that the
successions of worlds only fills us with sad astonishment. We should welcome with a more fraternal
and friendly eye the future of civilisation, and the
immediate destiny of our fellow men. The closer
at hand the future, the more we are concerned about
it. Unfortunately, moral and political sciences are
inaccurate, and full of uncertainty. They have but
an imperfect knowledge of the so far accomplished
developments of human evolution, and can therefore
not instruct us concerning the developments which
remain to be completed. Equipped with hardly any
memory, they have little or no presentiment. This
is why scientific minds feel an insurmountable re-
pugnance to attempt investigations, the uselessness
of which they know, and they dare not even confess
to a curiosity which they entertain no hope of
satisfying. Willingly would the task be undertaken

to discover what would happen, were men to become
wiser. Plato, Sir Thomas More, Campanella,
Fénelon, Cabet, and Paul Adam * have recon-
structed their particular city in Atlantis, in the is-
land of Utopia, in the Sun, at Salentinum, in Icaria,
in Malaya, and established there an abstract social
administration. Others, like the philosopher Sébas-
tien Mercier, and the socialist-poet William Morris,
dived into a far-off future. But they took their
system of morals with them. They discovered a
new Atlantis, and it is a city of dreamland which
they have harmoniously built there. Shall I also
quote Maurice Spronck? † He shows us the French
Republic conquered by the Moors, in the 230th
year of its foundation. He argues thus, in order
to induce us to hand over the government to the
Conservatives whom alone he considers capable of
warding off so great a disaster. Meanwhile Camille Mauclair,‡ trusting in humanity to come, reads
in the future the victorious resistance of Socialistic
Europe against Mussulman Asia. Daniel Halévy
dreads not the Moors, but, with greater show of
reason, the Russians. He narrates, in his *Histoire*

* Paul Adam, journalist and playwright; contributor to the
Revue de Paris and the *Nouvelle Revue.*

† Maurice Spronck, journalist and barrister; contributor to the
Journal des Débats, the *Revue des Deux Mondes,* the *Revue bleue,*
and the *Revue hebdomadaire.*

‡ Camille Faust, *dit* Camille Mauclair, art critic and lecturer;
author of works on Greuze, Fragonard, Schumann, Rodin, and
of *De Watteau à Whistler.*

de quatre ans, the foundation, in 2001, of the United States of Europe. But he seeks to show us more especially that the moral equilibrium of nations is unstable, and that a facility suddenly introduced into the conditions of life may suffice to let loose on a multitude of men the worst scourges and the most cruel sufferings.

"Few are those who have sought to know the future, out of pure curiosity, and without moral intention or optimistic designs. I know no other than H. G. Wells who, journeying through future ages, has discovered for humanity a fate he did not, according to every indication, expect; for the institution of an anthropophagous proletariat and an edible aristocracy is a cruel solution of social questions. Yet such is the fate H. G. Wells assigns to posterity. All the other prophets of whom I have any knowledge content themselves with entrusting to future centuries the realisation of their dreams. They do not unveil the future, being satisfied with conjuring it up.

"The truth is that men do not look so far ahead without fright. Many consider that such an investigation is not only useless, but pernicious; while those most ready to believe that future events are discoverable are those who would most dread to discover them. This fear is doubtless based on profound reasons. All morals, all religions, embody a revelation of humanity's destiny. The greater part of men, whether they admit it to, or conceal it from, themselves, would recoil from investigating these august revelations, to discover the emptiness of their anticipations.   They are accustomed to endure the idea of manners totally different from their own, if once those manners are buried in the past. Thereupon they congratulate themselves on the progress made by morality.   But, as their morality is in the main governed by their manners, or rather by what they allow one to see of them, they dare not confess to themselves that morality, which has continually changed with manners, up to their own day, will undergo a further change when they have passed out of this life, and that future men are liable to conceive an idea entirely at variance with their own as to what is permissible or not.   It would go against the grain with them to admit that their virtues are merely transitory, and their gods decrepit. And, although the past is there to point out to them ever-changing and shifting rights and duties, they would look upon themselves as dupes were they to foresee that future humanity is to create for itself new rights, duties and gods.   Finally, they fear disgracing themselves in the eyes of their contemporaries, in assuming the horrible immorality which future morality stands for.   Such are the obstacles to a quest of the future.   Look at Gallio and his friends; they would not have dared to foresee the equality of classes in the matter of marriage, the

abolition of slavery, the rout of the legions, the fall
of the Empire, the end of Rome, nor even the death
of those very gods in whom they had all but ceased
to believe."

" 'Tis possible," said Joséphin Leclerc, "but it is
time for us to dine."

And, leaving the Forum bathed in the calm light
of the moon, they wended their way through the
populous streets of the city towards a famed but
cheap eating-house in the Via Condotti.

IV

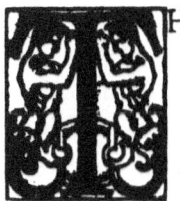HE room was small, and hung with a smoke-stained paper dating from the pontificate of Pio Nono. Ancient lithographs were dependent from the walls, representing Cavour with his tortoise-shell-framed spectacles and collar-like beard, the leonine visage of Garibaldi, the stupendous moustaches of Victor Emanuel, a classic placing side by side of the combined symbols of the revolution and of the supreme power, a popular testimony to the Italian spirit which excels in juxtapositions, and in whose midst, in our own day, in Rome, the fulminating Pope and the excommunicated King daily exchange assurances of good-neighbourship, with an exquisite grasp of politics, and not without a certain flavour of delicate comedy. The mahogany sideboard was laden with plated chafing-dishes and alabaster goblets. The establishment affected for new things a contempt appropriate to long-standing renown.

Seated around a table bedecked with roses, and with flasks of Chianti before them, the five continued their philosophic discourse.

"It is quite true," said Nicole Langelier, "that the heart fails in the case of many men, when gazing into the abyss of future events. It is moreover certain that our all too imperfect knowledge of facts past and gone does not supply us with the elements required to enable us to determine accurately what is to succeed them. However, since the past of human social organisations is in part known to us, the future of those societies, a continuation and consequence of their past, is not wholly beyond our ken. It is not impossible to observe certain social phenomena, and to define from the conditions under which they have already occurred, the conditions under which they will reappear. We are not barred, when witnessing the commencement of an order of facts, from comparing it with a past order of analogous facts, and from deducting from the completion of the second a like completion of the first. By way of example: when observing that the forms of labour are changeable, that serfdom has succeeded slavery, salaried labour, serfdom, new methods of production may be anticipated; when it is shown that industrial capital has for barely a century taken the place of the small artisans and peasant property, one is led to ponder over the form which is to succeed capital; when studying the manner in which was carried out the redemption of the feudal burdens and conditions of servitude, one is enabled to conceive how the redemption of the means of production nowadays constituting private ownership may some day be carried out. By studying the great Services of the State now in operation, it is possible to form a conception of future socialistic methods of production; and, after having thus investigated in several respects the present and the past of human industry, we shall, lacking certainties, determine by aid of probabilities whether collectivism is to be realized some day, not because it is just, for there is no reason for believing in the triumph of justice, but because it is the necessary sequel to the present state of things, and the fatal consequence of capitalistic evolution.

"Let us, if you like, take another example: we possess some experience of the life and death of religions. The end of Roman polytheism in particular, is familiar to us. Its lamentable end enables us to imagine that of Christianity, whose decline we are witnessing.

"We may similarly seek to find out whether future humanity will be bellicose or peaceful."

"I am curious to learn," said Joséphin Leclerc, "how to set about it."

M. Goubin shook his head, saying:

"Such a quest is useless. We know its result beforehand. War will last as long as the world."

"There is nothing to prove it," replied Langelier, "and a consideration of the past leads one to believe, on the contrary, that war is not one of the essential conditions of social life."

And Langelier, while waiting for the *minestra*

(soup) which was long in making its appearance, developed the foregoing idea, without, however, departing from the moderation characterising his mind.

"Although the early periods of the human race," he said, "are lost to us in impenetrable darkness, it is certain that men were not always warlike. They were not so during the long ages of the pastoral life; the memory of which survives only in a small number of words common to all Indo-European languages, and which reveal innocent manners. And there are reasons for believing that these peaceful pastoral centuries had a far longer duration than the agricultural, industrial, and commercial periods which, following them in a necessary progress, brought about between tribes and nations a state of all but constant war.

"It was by force of arms that it was most frequently sought to acquire property, lands, women, slaves, and cattle. At first, wars were waged between village and village. Next, the vanquished, joining hands with the victors, formed a nation, and wars occurred between nation and nation. Each of these peoples, in order to retain possession of the acquired riches, or to make further acquisitions, contended with neighbouring peoples for the possession of strongholds securing the command of roads, mountain passes, river courses, and the seashore. In the end, nations formed confederations, and contracted alliances. Thus it came about that men banded together; as they increased in strength, instead of contending for the goods of the earth, formally bartered them. The community of sentiments and interests gradully became broadened. A day came when Rome imagined she had established it the world over. Augustus thought he had inaugurated the era of universal peace.

"We know how this illusion was gradually and savagely dissipated, and how the barbarian hordes overwhelmed the Roman peace. These barbarians, who had settled within the Empire, cut one another's throats on its ruins, for a space of fourteen centuries, and founded in carnage countries baptized in blood. Of such was the life of nations in the Middle Ages, and the constitution of the great European monarchies.

"In those days, a state of war was alone possible and conceivable. All the forces of the world were organised solely for the purpose of maintaining it.

"If the reawakening of thought, at the time of the Renaissance, permitted a few sparse minds to conceive better regulated relations between nations, at one and the same time, the burning desire to invent, and the thirst for knowledge supplied fresh food to the warrior instinct. The discovery of the West Indies, the exploration of Africa, the navigation of the Pacific Ocean, opened up vast territories to European avidity. The white kingdoms joined issue over the extermination of the red, yellow, and black races, and for the space of four centuries gave themselves up madly to the pillaging of three great divisions of the world. This is what is styled modern civilisation.

"During this uninterrupted succession of deeds of rapine and violence, Europeans acquired a knowledge of the extent and configuration of the earth. As they progressed in this knowledge, so did their work of destruction proceed apace. To the present day, the whites come in contact with the black or the yellow races but to enslave or massacre them. The peoples whom we call barbarians know us so far through our crimes only.

"For all that, those navigations, those explorations undertaken in a spirit of savage cupidity, these tracks by land and by sea opened up to conquerors, adventures, hunters of and traders in men, these life-destroying colonisations, this brutal impulse which has led and still leads one-half of humanity to destroy the other, are the fatal conditions of a further progress of civilisation, and the terrible means which shall have prepared, for a still undetermined future, the peace of the world.

"This time, 'tis the whole world assimilated, in spite of enormous dissimilarities, to the state of the Roman Empire under Augustus. The Roman peace was the fruit of conquest. Universal peace will most assuredly not be brought about by the same

means. No Empire is there to-day which can lay
claim to the hegemony of the lands and seas covering the globe, known and surveyed at last. But,
in spite of their being less apparent than those of
political and military domination, the bonds which
are beginning to unite the whole of humanity, and
no longer merely a part of humanity, are none the
less real; they are both more supple and more solid;
more intimate and infinite in variety, since they are
connected, athwart the fictions of public life, with
the realities of social life.

"The increasing multiplicity of communications
and exchanges, the compulsory solidarity of the
financial markets of every capital, of commercial
markets vainly striving to guarantee their independ-
ence by recourse to unfortunate expedients, the
rapid growth of international socialism, seem likely
to guarantee, sooner or later, the union of the
peoples of every continent. If at the present moment the Imperialist spirit of the great States and
the haughty ambitions of armed nations seem to
give the lie to these previsions, and to damn these
aspirations, it will be perceived that in reality modern nationalism amounts merely to a confused as-
piration towards a more and more vast union of intellects and wills, and that the dream of a greater
England, a greater Germany, a greater America,
leads, will or do whatever you may, to the dream
of a greater humanity, and to a partnership between

nations for the common exploitation of the riches of the earth. . . ."

The speech was interrupted by the appearance of the tavern-keeper bearing a steaming soup-tureen and grated cheese.

And, from amid the hot and aromatic vapour of the soup, Nicole Langelier concluded his argument with these words:

"There will doubtless be further wars. The savage instincts coupled with the natural desires, pride and hunger, which have embroiled the world for so many centuries, will again disturb it. The human masses have so far not found their equilibrium. The sagacity of nations is not yet sufficiently methodical to secure the common welfare, by means of the freedom and the facility of exchanges, man has so far not come to be looked up to with respect everywhere by man, the several portions of humanity are not yet about to associate harmoniously for the purpose of building the cells and organs of one and the same body. It will not be vouchsafed even unto the youngest of us to witness the close of the era of arms. But, we feel within us a presentiment of these better times which we are not to experience. If we extend into the future the present trend, we may even now determine the establishment of more perfect and frequent communications between all races and all nations, a more general and stronger feeling of human solidarity, the rational organisation of labour, and the coming of the United States of the World.

"Universal peace will become a fact some day, not because men will become better ('tis more than we may hope for), but because a new order of things, a new science, and new economic necessities will force on men the state of peace, just as formerly the very conditions of their existence placed and kept them in a state of war."

"Nicole Langelier, a rose has shed a leaf in your glass," said Giacomo Boni. "This has not taken place without the permission of the gods. Let us drink to the future peace of the world."

Raising his glass, Joséphin Leclerc remarked:

"This wine of Chianti has a tart savour, and a light sparkle. Let us drink to peace, the while Russians and Japanese are waging a bitter war in Manchuria and in Korea Bay."

"That war," resumed Langelier, "marks one of the great periods in the history of the world. And, in order to grasp its meaning, we must hark back two thousand years.

"The Romans, assuredly, did not suspect the vastness of the barbarian world, and had no conception of those immense human reservoirs which were to burst on them one fine day, and submerge them. They did not suspect that there existed in the world any other than the Roman peace. And yet, an older and vaster one there was, the Chinese peace.

"Not but what their merchants had business relations with the merchants of Serica. The latter were wont to bring raw silk to a spot situated to the north of the Pamir table-land, named the Tower of Stone. The merchants of the Empire went thither. Bolder Latin traders penetrated as far as the Gulf of Tong-King and the Chinese coasts up to Hang-chau-fu, or Hanoi. Nevertheless, the Romans did not conceive that Serica constituted an Empire more densely populated than their own one, richer, and more advanced in agriculture and political economy. The Chinese, on their part, knew the white men. Their annals mention the fact that the Emperor An-tung, under which name we recognise Marcus Aurelius Antoninus, despatched an embassy to them, which was perhaps merely an expedition of navigators and merchants. But they were ignorant of the fact that a civilisation more seething and violent than their own, as well as more prolific and infinitely more expansive, was spread over one of the faces of the globe of which they covered another face: the Chinese, agriculturists and gardeners full of experience, honest and expert merchants, led a happy life, owing to their system of exchange and to their immense associations of credit. Contented with their subtle science, their exquisite politeness, their singularly human piety, and their immutable wisdom, they were doubtless not anxious to become acquainted with the ways of life and thought of the white men who had come from the land of Cæsar. Perchance the ambassadors of An-tung may have seemed somewhat gross and barbarian to them.

"The two great civilisations, the yellow and the white, continued ignorant of each other until the day when the Portuguese, having doubled the Cape of Good Hope, settled down to trade at Macao. Merchants and Christian missionaries established themselves in China, and indulged in every kind of violence and rapine. The Chinese tolerated them, in the manner of men accustomed to works of patience, and marvellously capable of endurance; nevertheless, they could on occasion take life with all the refinements of cruelty. For nearly three whole centuries the Jesuits were, in the Middle Kingdom, a source of endless disturbances. In our own times, the Christian acquired the habit of sending jointly or separately into that vast Empire, whenever order was disturbed, soldiers who restored it by means of theft, rape, pillage, murder, and incendiarism, and of proceeding at short intervals with the pacific penetration of the country with rifles and guns. The poorly armed Chinese either defend themselves badly or not at all, and so they are massacred with delightful facility. They are polite and ceremonious, but are reproached with cherishing feeble sentiments of affection for Europeans. The grievances we have against them are greatly of the order of those which Mr. Du Chaillu cherished towards his gorilla. Mr. Du Chaillu, while in a forest, brought down with his rifle the mother of a gorilla. In its death, the brute was still pressing its young to its bosom. He tore it from this embrace, and dragged it with him in a cage across Africa, for the purpose of selling it in Europe. Now, the young animal gave him just cause for complaint. It was unsociable, and actually starved itself to death. 'I was powerless,' says Mr. Du Chaillu, 'to correct its evil nature.' We complain of the Chinese with as great a show of reason as Mr. Du Chaillu of his gorilla.

"In 1901, order having been disturbed at Peking, the troops of the five Great Powers, under the command of a German Field-Marshal, restored it by the customary means. Having in this fashion covered themselves with military glory, the five Powers signed one of the innumerable treaties by which they guarantee the integrity of the very China whose provinces they divide among themselves.

"Russia's share was Manchuria, and she closed Korea to Japanese trade. Japan, which in 1894 had beaten the Chinese on land and on sea, and had taken a part, in 1901, in the pacifying action of the Powers, saw with concentrated fury the advance of

the voracious and slow-footed she-bear.   And, while
the huge brute indolently stretched out its muzzle
towards the Japanese beehive, the yellow bees,
arming their wings and stings together, riddled it
with burning punctures.

" 'It is a colonial war,' was the expression used by
a high-placed Russian official to my friend Georges
Bourdon.*   Now, the fundamental principle of
every colonial war is that the European should be
more powerful than the peoples whom he is fighting;
this is as clear as noonday.   It is understood that in
these kinds of wars the European is to attack with
artillery, while the Asiatic or African is of course
to defend himself with arrows, clubs, assegais and
tomahawks.   It is tolerated that he should procure
a few antiquated flint-locks and cartridge-pouches;
this aids in rendering colonisation more glorious.
But in no case is it permissible that he should be
armed and instructed in European fashion.   His
fleet must consist of junks, canoes and 'dug-outs.'
Should he perchance purchase ships from European
ship-owners, such ships shall naturally be unfit for
use.   The Chinese who fill their arsenals with porce-
lain shells conform to the rules of colonial warfare.

"The Japanese have departed from these rules.
They wage war in accordance with the principles
taught in France by General Bonnal.   They greatly

* M. Georges Bourdon, journalist, on the staff of *Le Figaro*.

outweighed their adversaries in knowledge and intelligence.   While fighting better than Europeans, they show no respect for consecrated usages, and act to a certain degree in a fashion contrary to the law of nations.

" 'Tis in vain that serious individuals like Monsieur Edmond Théry * demonstrated to them that they were bound to be beaten, in the superior interest of the European market and in conformity with the most firmly established economic laws. Vainly did the proconsul of Indo-China, Monsieur Doumer himself, call upon them to suffer, and at short notice, decisive defeats on sea and on land. 'What a financial sadness would bow down our hearts,' exclaimed this great man, 'were Bezobrazoff and Alexeieff not to extract another million out of the Korean forests.   They are kings. Like them, I was a king: our cause is a common one.   Oh ye Japanese!   Imitate in their gentleness the copper-coloured folk over whom I reigned so gloriously under Méline.'   In vain did Dr. Charles Richet,† skeleton in hand, represent to them that being prognathous, and not having the muscles of their calves sufficiently developed, they were under

* M. Edmond Théry, journalist, on the staff of *Le Figaro*. Has been entrusted by the French Government with several politico-economic missions; author of several works in this connection.

† Dr. Charles Richet, a noted physician, who has written plays, and is the author of several works on physiology and sociology.

the obligation of seeking flight in the trees when face to face with the Russians, who are brachy-cephalous and as such eminently civilising, as was demonstrated when they drowned five thousand Chinese in the Amur. 'Bear in mind that you are links between monkey and man,' obligingly said to them my Lord Professor Richet, 'as a consequence of which, if you should defeat the Russians or Finno-Letto-Ugro-Slavs, it would be exactly as if monkeys were to beat you. Is it not plain to you?' They heeded him not.

"At the present moment, the Russians are paying the penalty, in the waters of Japan and in the gorges of Manchuria, not only of their grasping and brutal policy in the East, but of the colonial policy of all Europe. They are now expiating, not merely their own crimes, but those of the whole of military and commercial Christianity. When saying this, I do not mean to say that there is a justice in the world. But we witness a strange whirligig of things, and brute force, up to now the sole judge of human ac-tions, indulges occasionally in unexpected pranks. Its sudden starts aside destroy an equilibrium thought to be stable. And its pranks, which are ever the work of some hidden rule, bring about in-teresting results. The Japanese cross the Yalu and defeat the Russians in good form. Their sailors an-nihilate artistically a European fleet. Immediately do we discern that a danger threatens us. If it indeed exists, who created it? It was not the Japanese who sought out the Russians. It was not the yellow men who hunted up the whites. We there and then make the discovery of a Yellow Peril. For many long years have Asiatics been familiar with the White Peril. The looting of the Summer Palace, the massacres of Pekin, the drownings of Blagovestchenk, the dismemberment of China, were these not enough to alarm the Chinese? As to the Japanese, could they feel secure under the guns of Port Arthur? We created the White Peril. The White Peril has engendered the Yellow Peril. We have here concatenations giving to the ancient Necessity which rules the world an appearance of divine Justice, and must perforce admire the astonishing behaviour of that blind queen of men and gods, when seeing Japan, formerly so cruel to the Chinese and Koreans, and the unpaid accessory to the crimes of Europeans in China, become the avenger of China, and the hope of the yellow race.

"It does not, however, appear at first sight that the Yellow Peril at which European economists are terrified is to be compared to the White Peril suspended over Asia. The Chinese do not send to Paris, Berlin, and St. Petersburg missionaries to teach Christians the Fung-chui, and sow disorder in European affairs. A Chinese expeditionary force did not land in Quiberon Bay to demand of the Government of the Republic *extra-territoriality, i. e.,* the right of trying by a tribunal of mandarins cases pending between Chinese and Europeans. Admiral Togo did not come and bombard Brest roads with a dozen battleships, for the purpose of improving Japanese trade in France. The flower of French nationalism, the *élite* of our Trublions, did not besiege in their mansions in the Avenues Hoche and Marceau the Legations of China and of Japan, and Marshal Oyama did not, for the same reason, lead the combined armies of the Far East to the Boulevard de la Madeleine to demand the punishment of the foreigner-hating Trublions. He did not burn Versailles in the name of a higher civilisation. The armies of the Great Asiastic Powers did not carry away to Tokio and Peking the Louvre paintings and the silver service of the Élysée.

"No indeed! Monsieur Edmond Théry himself admits that the yellow men are not sufficiently civilised to imitate the whites so faithfully. Nor does he foresee that they will ever rise to so high a moral culture. How could it be possible for them to possess our virtues? They are not Christians. But men entitled to speak consider that the Yellow Peril is none the less to be dreaded for all that it is economic. Japan, and China organised by Japan, threaten us, in all the markets of Europe, with a competition frightful, monstrous, enormous, and deformed, the mere idea of which causes the hair of the economists to stand on end. That is why

Japanese and Chinese must be exterminated. There
can be no doubt about the matter. But war must
also be declared against the United States to pre-
vent it from selling iron and steel at a lower price
than our manufacturers less well equipped in machinery.

"Let us for once admit the truth, and for a
moment cease flattering ourselves. Our Europe and
new Europe—for that is America's true name—
have inaugurated economic war. Each and every
nation is waging an industrial struggle against the
others. Everywhere does production arm itself
furiously against production. We are displaying
bad grace when we complain that we are witnessing
fresh competing and disturbing products invade the
market of the world thus thrown into confusion.
Of what use are our lamentations? That might is
right is our god. If Tokio is the weaker, it shall
be in the wrong and it shall be made to feel it; if it
is the stronger, right will be on its side, and we shall
have no reproach to cast at it. Where is the nation in the world entitled to speak in the name of
justice?

"We have taught the Japanese both the capitalistic *régime* and war. They are a cause of alarm
because they are becoming like ourselves. In truth,
it is awful. They dare to defend themselves with
European weapons against Europeans. Their generals, their naval officers, who have studied in Eng-

В

land, in Germany, and in France, reflect honour on the instructors. Several of them have followed the classes of our special military schools. The Russian Grand Dukes, who feared that no good could come out of military institutions too democratic to their taste, must feel reassured.

"I am unable to foretell the issue of the war. The Russian Empire opposes to the methodical energy of the Japanese its irresolute forces which the savage imbecility of its government restrains, the dishonesty of a voracious administration robs, and military incapacity leads to disaster. The stupendousness of its impotence and the depths of its disorganisation stand revealed. Withal, its golden reservoirs, kept filled by its rich creditors, are all but inexhaustible. On the other hand, its enemy has no other resources than onerous loans obtained with difficulty, of which victory itself may perchance deprive them. For while English and Americans are one in assisting it to weaken Russia, they do not intend that it shall become powerful and to be feared. It is hard to predict the final victory of one combatant over the other. But if Japan makes the yellow men respected by the white men, it will have greatly served the cause of humanity, and paved the way unawares and doubtless against its own wish for the pacific organization of the world."

"What do you mean," said M. Goubin, raising

his eyes from his plate filled with a savoury *fritto*.

"It is feared," continued Nicole Langelier, "that Japan grown to manhood will educate China, teach it to defend itself and to exploit its wealth itself, and that Japan will create a strong China. No need to look upon such a contingency with alarm; it should, on the contrary, be hoped for in the universal interest. Strong nations co-operate to the harmony and wealth of the world. Weak nations, like China and Turkey, are a perpetual cause of disturbances and perils. But we are ever in too great a haste in our fears and hopes. Should victorious Japan undertake to organise the old yellow Empire, it will not succeed in its task that quickly. It will require time to teach China that a China exists. For she knows it not, and as long as she is unaware of it, there will not be any China. A people exists only in the knowledge possessed by it of its existence. There are 350,000,000 Chinese, but they are not aware of the fact. As long as they have not counted themselves, they will not count for anything. They will not even exist by dint of numbers. 'Number off!' is the first word of command spoken by the drill-sergeant to his men. He is there and then teaching them the principle of societies. But it takes a long time for 350,000,000 men to number themselves. Nevertheless, Ular, who is a European out of the common, since he believes that one should be humane and just towards

the Chinese, informs us that a great national movement is simmering in all the provinces of the huge
empire."

"And even should it happen," said Joséphin
Leclerc, "that victorious Japan came to infuse into
Mongols, Chinese, and Tibetans a consciousness of
themselves, and caused them to be respected by the
white races, in what way would the peace of the
world be better assured, and the conquering mania
of nations be kept within stricter bounds? Would
not negro humanity still remain to be exterminated?
Where is the black nation which will insure the
respecting of negroes by the white and yellow
races?"

"But," interposed Nicole Langelier, "who can
define how far one of the great human races may
go? The blacks are not, like the red man, dying
out through contact with the Europeans. Where
is the prophet who will venture to tell the 200,000,-
000 African blacks that their posterity will never enjoy wealth and peace on the lakes and great rivers?
The white men passed through the ages of caves
and lucustrine villages. They were at that time
wild and naked. They dried rude potteries in the
sun. Their chiefs led barbarian dances at which
they shouted. They knew no other sciences than
those of their sorcerers. Since those days they
have built the Parthenon, conceived geometry,
subjected the expression of their thought and

the motions of their body to the laws of harmony. "Are you then going to say to the African negroes: 'You shall for ever carry on an internecine war between tribe and tribe, and you shall inflict upon one another atrocities and absurd tortures; King Gléglé, permeated with a religious idea, shall for all time have prisoners tied up in a basket and thrown from the roof of his royal hut; you shall for ever devour with enjoyment the strips of flesh torn from the decomposed cadavers of your aged relations; for ever shall explorers unload their rifles on you, and smoke you out in your kraals; the wonderful Christian soldier will enjoy in his bravery the amusement of hacking your women to pieces; the gay and festive sailor from the befogged seas shall for all time kick in the bellies of your little children, just to take the stiffness out of his knee-joints? Can you safely prophesy to one-third of humanity a state of perpetual ignominy?

"I am unable to say whether one day, as Mrs. Beecher Stowe predicted in 1840, a life will awaken in Africa full of a splendour and magnificence unknown to the cold-blooded races of the West, and whether art will blossom forth in new and dazzling forms. The blacks possess a keen appreciation of music. It may happen that a delightful negro art dance and song shall see the light of day. In the meanwhile, the coloured folk of the Southern States are making rapid strides in capitalistic civilisation.

Monsieur Jean Finot * has recently supplied us with information on the subject.

"Fifty years ago they did not, as a whole, own two hundred and fifty acres of land. Nowadays their property is valued at over £160,000,000. They were illiterate. To-day fifty per cent. of them can read and write. There are black novelists, poets, economists, and philanthropists.

"The half-breeds, the issue of master and slave, are singularly intelligent and vigorous. The coloured men, both cunning and ferocious, instinctive and calculating, will gradually (so one of them has confided to me) reap the advantage of number, and one day lord it over the effeminate creole race which exercises so lightly over the blacks its fitful cruelty. It may be that the mulatto of genius, who will make the children of the whites pay dearly the blood of the negroes lynched by their fathers, is already born."

M. Goubin primed himself with his powerful eye-glass, and remarked:

"Were the Japanese to be victorious, they would take Indo-China from us."

"Thereby rendering us a great service," answered Langelier. "Colonies are the curse of nations."

M. Goubin's indignant silence was his sole reply.

"I cannot listen to such statements," exclaimed

* M. Jean Finot, editor of *La Revue,* and contributor to several French and European publications.

Joséphin Leclerc. "We require outlets for our products, and territories for our industrial and commercial expansion. What are you thinking of, Langelier? One policy alone governs Europe, America, and the world to-day—colonial policy."

Nicole Langelier, unruffled, replied:

"Colonial policy is the most recent form of barbarism, or, if you prefer, the term of civilisation. I make no distinction between these two expressions; they are identical. What men call civilisation is the present condition of manners, while what they style barbarism are anterior conditions. The manners of to-day will be styled barbarian when they shall be of the past. It is patent to me that our manners and morals embody the idea that strong nations shall destroy the weaker ones. Of such is the principle of the law of nations.

"It remains to be seen, however, whether conquests abroad always constitute a good stroke of business for nations. It would not seem so. What have Mexico and Peru done for Spain? Brazil for Portugal? Batavia for Holland? There are various kinds of colonies. There are colonies which afford to unfortunate Europeans desert and uncultivated lands. These, loyal as long as they remain poor, separate from the mother country as soon as they become prosperous. Some there are which are inhabitable; these supply raw material, and import manufactured goods. Now it is plain that these colonies enrich, not those who govern them, but whoever trades with them. The greater part of the time they are not worth what they cost. Moreover, they may at any moment expose the mother country to military disasters."

"How about England?" interrupted M. Goubin.

"England is less a nation than a race. The Anglo-Saxons know no fatherland but the sea. England, looked upon as wealthy in her vast domains, owes her fortune and her power to her commerce. It is not her colonies which should be envied her, but her merchants, the authors of her wealth. Do you imagine, by way of illustration, that the Transvaal represents so very good a stroke of business for her? For all that, it is conceivable that in the present state of the world nations who bring forth many children and manufacture products in large quantities should seek territories and markets in far-off lands, and secure possession of them by stratagem and violence. How different it is in our own case! Our thrifty nation, careful not to have more children than the natal soil can feed without difficulty, and producing in a moderate degree, does not willingly embark on distant adventures; our France, who hardly goes beyond her garden wall, great heavens, what need has she of colonies? Of what use are they to her? What do they bring her? She has spent men and money in profusion, in order that the Congo, Cochin-China,

Annam, Tonking, Guiana, and Madagascar shall
purchase calicoes from Manchester, guns from
Birmingham and Liège, brandies from Dantzig,
and cases of wine all the way from Bordeaux to
Hamburg. She has, for seventy years, despoiled,
hunted, and shot down Arabs, and in the end she
has peopled Algeria with Italians and Spaniards!

"The irony of these results is cruel enough, and
it is hard to realise that this empire, ten or eleven
times as big as France herself, has been formed to
our detriment. But, it must be taken into consideration that whereas the French nation derives
no advantage whatsoever from the possession of
territories in Africa and Asia, the heads of its
Government, on the other hand, find it to their
great advantage to acquire them. They thereby
secure the affection of the navy and army, which on
the occasion of colonial expeditions reap a harvest
of promotions, pensions, and crosses, to say nothing
of the glory won in defeating the enemy. They
conciliate the clergy by opening new paths to the
Propaganda, and by allocating territories to Cath-
olic missions. They make joyous the ship-owners,
builders, and army contractors, whom they load with
orders. They secure for themselves in the country
itself a numerous following by the granting of con-
cessions of immense forests and plantations without
end. And, what is still more precious to them,
they attach to their majority every parliamentary

jobber and kerbstone-broker. Lastly, they cajole
the multitude, proud in its possession of a yellow
and black empire, which makes Germany and England turn green with envy. They are looked upon
as good citizens, patriots, and great statesmen.
And if, like Ferry, they incur the risk of going
under, as the result of some military disaster, they
willingly run the risk fully convinced that the most
harmful of distant expositions will cost them fewer
difficulties, and will inveigle them into fewer perils
than the most useful of social reforms.

"You can now realise why we have occasionally
had imperialist ministers, jealous of aggrandising
our colonial domain. We must congratulate ourselves, however, and praise the moderation of our
rulers, who might have burdened us with still more
colonies.

"But all danger has not been averted, and we are
threatened with an eighty years' warfare in Mo-
rocco.   Is there never to be an end to the colonial
mania?

"I am fully aware that nations are not sensible.
How can it be expected of them, if one considers
what they are made of? Still, a certain instinct
oftentimes warns them of what is harmful. They
are occasionally endowed with the power of observing. In the long run they undergo the painful experience of their errors and blunders. The day
will come when it will dawn upon them that colonies

are a source of perils and ruinous results. Commercial barbarism will be followed by commercial civilisation, and forcible, by pacific penetration. These ideas have to-day found an echo even in the bosom of parliaments. They will prevail, not because men will be more disinterested, but because they will know their own interests better.

"The great human asset is man himself. In order to rate the terrestrial globe, it is necessary to begin by rating men. To exploit the soil, the mines, the waters, all the substances and all the forces of our planet, it needs man, the whole of man; humanity, the whole of humanity. The complete exploitation of the terrestrial globe demands the united labour of white, yellow, and black men. By reducing, diminishing, and weakening, or, to sum it up in one word, by colonising a portion of humanity, we are working against ourselves. It is to our advantage that yellow and black men should be powerful, free, and wealthy. Our prosperity and our wealth depend on theirs. The more is produced, the more will there be consumed. The greater the profit they derive from us, the greater the profit we shall derive from them. If they reap the benefit of our labours, so shall we fully reap theirs.

"If we study the movements which govern the destinies of societies, we may perhaps discover signs that the era of violent deeds is coming to an end.

War, which was formerly a standing institution among nations, is now intermittent, and the periods of peace have become of longer duration than those of war. Our country affords the observations of a fact full of interest, for the French nation presents an original characteristic in the military history of nations. Whereas other nations never waged war except from interest or necessity, alone the French have fought for the pleasure of fighting. Now it is remarkable that the taste of our compatriots has undergone a change. Thirty years ago Renan wrote: 'Whoever knows France as a whole and in her provincial varieties will not hesitate to recognise the fact that the movement swaying this country for the past fifty years is essentially pacific.' It is a fact attested by a large number of observers that in 1870 France had no desire to have recourse to the arbitrament of war, and that the declaration of war was greeted with consternation. It is an assured fact that few Frenchmen dream of taking the field, and that everybody readily accepts the idea that the army exists in order to avoid a war. Let me quote one example out of a thousand in confirmation of this state of mind. Monsieur Ribot, a representative of the people and a former Cabinet Minister, having been invited to some patriotic celebration, replied with an eloquent letter, begging to be excused. The same Monsieur Ribot knits his brows superciliously at the mere mention of the

word disarmament. He has towards standards
and cannon the leaning proper to a former Minister of Foreign Affairs.   In his letter he denounces
as a national peril the pacific ideas disseminated by
the Socialist.   He sees in them a spirit of renuncia-
tion he cannot endure.   Not that he is of a bellicose turn of mind.   He, too, sighs for peace, but
a peace full of pomp, magnificent, and flashing with
the same pride as war.   Between Monsieur Ribot
and Jaurès, the matter is merely one of form.
Both of them are for peace.   Jaurès, simply; Monsieur Ribot, superbly.   That is all.   Better still
and more surely than the Socialist democracy which
contents itself with a bloused or coated peace does
the sentiment of the bourgeois, who demand a
peace gleaming with military insignia and bedecked
with emblems of glory, testify to the inevitable decline of all idea of revenge and conquests, since one
discerns in it the military instinct, at the very time
when it is losing its nature and is becoming pacific.

"France is acquiring by degrees the sentiment of
her true strength, consisting in intellectual strength;
she is becoming conscious of her mission, which is
the sowing of ideas and the exercise of a sway over
thought.   She will within measurable time perceive
that her only stable power has lain in her speakers,
her writers, and her men of science.   Hence she
will some day fain have to recognise that the force
of numbers, after having so often betrayed her, is

finally escaping from her, and that the time has
come for her to resign herself to the glory which
the exercise of the mind and the use of reason assure
her of."

Jean Boilly, shaking his head, said:

"You ask that France should teach other nations
concord and peace. Are you so sure that she will
be listened to and her example followed? Is her
own tranquillity so assured? Has she not to fear
threats from outside, to foresee dangers, to watch
over her safety, and to provide for her defence?
One swallow does not make a summer; one nation
does not make the peace of the world. Is it so
sure that Germany keeps up an army with the sole
object of not waging war? Her Social-Democrats
desire peace. But they are not the masters, and
their deputies do not enjoy in the Parliament the
authority which the number of their electors should
give them. And Russia, who has hardly entered
upon the industrial period, do you believe that she
will soon be entering upon the pacific period? Is it
not to be feared that after having disturbed Asia
she will disturb Europe?

"Supposing even that Europe should become
pacific, can you not see that America would become
warlike? Follow upon Cuba, reduced to the state
of a vassal republic, Hawaii, Porto Rico, and the
annexation of the Philippines, it is impossible to say
that the American Union is not a conquering nation.

A publicist of Yankee proclivities, Stead, has said
amid the plaudits of the whole of the United States:
'The Americanisation of the world is on the march.'
And then there is Mr. Roosevelt, whose dream is
to plant the Stars and Stripes in South Africa,
Australia, and the West Indies. Mr. Roosevelt is
Imperialist and he sighs for an American mistress
of the world. Between ourselves, he is planning
the Empire of Augustus. He has unfortunately
perused Livy. The conquests of the Romans
banish sleep from him. Have you read his
speeches? They breathe a bellicose spirit. 'Fight,
my friends,' says Mr. Roosevelt, 'and fight hard.
There is nothing like blows. We are upon earth
only to exterminate one another. Those who tell
you the contrary are men without morality. Mis-
trust men who think. Thought enervates. 'Tis a
French failing. The Romans conquered the world.
They lost it. We are the modern Romans.'
Words full of eloquence, backed up with a navy
which will soon be the second in the world, and with
a military Budget of 40,500,000 francs!

"The Yankees declare that in four years' time
they will fight Germany. If we are to believe this,
they should first tell us where they expect to come
into contact with the enemy. That a Russia, the
serf of her Czar, that a still feudal Germany, should
entertain armies for fighting purposes, this one is

tempted to lay to the door of ancient habits and the survival of a strenuous past. But that a young democracy, the United States of America, an aggregation of business men, a mass of emigrants from all countries, lacking community, traditions, and memories, madly cast into the scramble for the mighty dollar, should of a sudden be swept with the desire of firing torpedoes at the flanks of battleships, and of exploring mines under the enemy's columns, affords a proof that the inordinate struggle for the production and exploitation of riches keeps alive the employment of and taste for brutal force, that industrial violence engenders military violence, and that mercantile rivalries kindle between nations hatreds that bloodshed can alone extinguish. The colonial mania of which you were speaking a while ago is but one of the thousand forms of the much-vaunted competition of our economists. The capitalistic state is just as much a warlike one as the feudal. The era has dawned of great wars for the industrial sovereignty. Under the present *régime* of national production it is the cannon which fixes tariffs, establishes customs, opens and closes markets. There exists no other regulator of commerce and industry. Extermination is the fatal result of the economic conditions in which the civilised world finds itself to-day. . . ."

The perfume of Gorgonzola and Stracchino was

pervading the table. The waiter was bringing in
wax-candles to each of which was attached the
abbrustolatoio * wherewith to light the long cigars
with straws, so dear to Italians.

Hippolyte Dufresne, who for some time past
seemed to have remained indifferent to the conversation, here remarked in a low tone tinged with
an ostentatious modesty:

"Gentlemen, our friend Langelier was asserting
just now that many men are afraid of disgracing
themselves in the eyes of their contemporaries by
assuming the horrible immorality which is to be the
morality of the future. I do not entertain a like
fear, and I have written a little tale, which has perhaps no other merit than the one revealing my
calmness of mind when considering the future. I
shall one day crave permission to read it to you."

"Read it right away," said Boni, lighting his
cigar.

"You will be giving us pleasure," added Joséphin
Leclerc, Nicole Langelier, and M. Goubin.

"I am not sure whether I have the manuscript
with me," replied Hippolyte Dufresne.

With these words, he drew out of his pocket a
roll of paper, and began to read what follows.

* *Abbrustolatoio*—apparatus attached to the candle; it has two
rings through which the cigar is placed, and left to burn awhile.

V

THROUGH THE HORN OR THE IVORY GATE

"T was about one o'clock in the morning. Before retiring for the night, I opened the window and lit a cigarette. The hum of a motor-car scudding along the Avenue du Bois de Boulogne broke the reigning silence. The trees were freshening the atmosphere by the swaying of their darkened tops. No buzzing insect, no living sound arose from the sterile soil of the city. The night was resplendent with stars. Their fires seemed, in the clearness of the air, more so than on other nights, of varied lines. The greater number blazed at white heat. Some there were, however, yellow and orange-tinted, similar to the flames of dying lamps. Several were blue, and I saw one of so pale a blue, so limpid, and so soft, that I could not avert my gaze from it. I regret being ignorant of its name, but I console myself with the thought that men do not give the stars their true names.

"When I reflect that each one of these drops of light enlightens worlds, I ask myself whether, like our own sun, they do not shed their rays on sufferings without end, and whether pain does not penetrate the utmost recesses of heaven. We can only judge the other worlds by our own. We know of life only the forms which it assumes upon the earth, and if we suppose that our planet is one of the least good, we have no reason for believing that all goes rightly in the others, nor that fortunate is he who is born under the rays of Altair, Betelgeux, or the fiery Sirius, when we know what a grievous affair it is to open our eyes on earth to the light of our old Sun. It is not that I find mine an unhappy fate, when compared with that of other men. I am not troubled with either wife or child. Love and sickness have left me unscathed. I am not very rich, and I do not go into society. I am thus to be numbered with the happy ones. Little joy, however, falls to their lot. What, then, can be the fate of the others? Men are really to be pitied. I impute no blame to nature for this; to hold a conversation with her is an impossibility; she is not intelligent. Nor will I lay the blame on society. There is no sense in opposing society to nature. It is as absurd to oppose the nature of men to the society of men, as to oppose the nature of ants to the society of ants, or the nature of herrings to the society of herrings. Animal societies are the necessary outcome of animal nature. The earth is the planet where one eats; 'tis the planet of hunger. The animals peopling it are naturally gluttonous and ferocious. Man, the most intelligent of them

all, is alone avaricious. Avarice has so far been
the fundamental virtue of human societies, and the
moral masterpiece of nature. Were I a writer, I
should indite the praise of avarice. It is true that
my book would not reveal anything strikingly new.
The subject has been dealt with a hundred times
over by moralists and economists. Human societies
have avarice and cruelty as their august basis.

"It is thus in the other universes, in the number-
less ethereal worlds? Do all the stars I see shed
their light on men? Do people eat and inter-
devour one another beyond the infinite. This
doubt troubles me, and I am unable to contemplate
without fright the fiery dew suspended in the
heavens.

"My thoughts imperceptibly become more lucid
and gentle, and the idea of life, in its sensuality,
violent and suave in turn, once more assumes a
pleasurable aspect to my mind. I sometimes say to
myself that life is beautiful. For, without such
beauty, how could we discern its ugly features, and
how believe that nature is bad, if at the same time
we do not believe that it is good?

"For a few minutes past, the phrases of a sonata
of Mozart have hovered in the air, with their white
columns and their garlands of roses. My neighbour
is a pianist, who at nights plays Mozart and Gluck.
I close the window, and while undressing, I am
pondering over the doubtful pleasures which I may

give myself the next day, when of a sudden I remember that for a week past I have been invited to lunch in the Bois de Boulogne; I have a vague idea that the invitation is for the coming day. To make sure of it, I look up the letter of invitation, which lies open on my table. Its contents are:

" '16th September 1903.
" 'My dear old Dufresne,—
" 'Do me the pleasure of coming to luncheon with . . . etc. etc., next Saturday, the 23rd of September, 1903, etc. etc.'

"It is for to-morrow.
"I ring for my valet.
" 'Jean, wake me to-morrow at nine o'clock.'
"It happens precisely that to-morrow, the 23rd of September 1903, I shall enter upon my fortieth year. From what I have already seen in this world I can almost conceive what still remains for me to be seen. I can safely foretell the topics of to-morrow's conversation at the restaurant in the Bois: 'My automobile goes sixty kilomètres an hour.'—'Blanche has a nasty disposition; but she is true to me; of that I feel sure.'—'The Cabinet takes its pass-word from the Socialists.'—'In the long run, the *petits-chevaux* are a bore. However, there remains *baccara*.'—'The workmen would be fools not to do as they please: the government always gives in to them.'—'I will bet you that Epingle-

d'Or will beat Ranavalo.'—'What I personally cannot make out is why there is not some General to
sweep away all those blackguards.'—'What can
you expect? France has been sold to England and
Germany by the Jews.' This is what I shall hear
to-morrow. Here you have the social and political
ideas of my friends, the great-grandsons of the
bourgeois of July, princes of the factory and foundry, kings of the mine, who knew the way of
mastering and enslaving the forces of the Revolution. My friends do not seem to me capable of
preserving for any lengthy period the industrial
empire and the political power bequeathed to them
by their ancestors. My friends do not shine by
their intelligence. They have not indulged in too
much brainwork. No more have I. So far, I have
not done much in this life. Like them, I am both
idle and ignorant. I do not feel myself capable of
achieving anything, and if I do not possess their
vanity, if my brain is not stored with all the foolish
ideas encumbering theirs; if, like them, I do not
feel a hatred for and a fear of ideas, it is due to a
peculiar circumstance of my life. My father, a big
manufacturer and Conservative deputy, gave me,
when I was seventeen, a young and timid 'coach,'
who spoke little, and who looked like a girl. While
preparing me for my bachelorship, he was organ-
ising the social revolution in Europe. His gentleness was something refreshing. He has often been

put in prison, and is now a deputy.   I used to copy his addresses to the international proletariat.   He made me read the whole Socialistic library.   He taught me things all of which were not to be credited, but he opened my eyes to what was going on about me; he demonstrated to me that everything our society honours is contemptible, and that all that it despises is worthy of esteem.   He led me into the paths of rebellion.   In spite of his demonstrations, I came to the conclusion that falsehood should be respected and hypocrisy venerated as the two surest supports of the public order.   I remained a Conservative, but my soul became saturated with disgust.

"As I am falling asleep, a few almost imperceptible phrases of Mozart still reach my ears now and then, and make me dream of temples of marble standing amid a blue foliage.

"It was broad daylight when I awoke.   I dressed myself much more quickly than it is my wont.   Unconscious of the cause for this haste, I found myself in the street without knowing how I had got there.   What I now saw about me was to me the cause of a surprise which suspended all my faculties of reflection; and it is owing to this impossibility to reflect that my surprise did not increase, but remained stationary and calm.   It would doubtless soon have become immoderate, and would have changed to stupor and terror, had I retained the use of my mind, so greatly was the scene which I was witnessing different from what it should be. Everything about me was to me new, unknown, and foreign. The trees and the lawns which I was in the habit of seeing daily had vanished. Where, on the day before, the tall grey buildings of the avenue stood out against the sky, there now stretched a fanciful line of brick cottages surrounded by gardens. I dared not look round to ascertain whether my own house still existed, and so I went straight towards the Porte Dauphine. I found it not. I took a street which was, so it seemed to me, the old road to Suresnes. The houses flanking it, of strange style and new form, too small to be occupied by rich people, were nevertheless embellished with pictures, sculptures, and brilliant potteries. A covered terrace surmounted them. I followed this rural road, whose curves produced enchanting perspectives. It was crossed obliquely by other sinuous ways. Neither trains, nor automobiles, nor vehicles of any kind went by. Shadows flitted over the soil. I looked upwards and saw masses of huge birds and enormous fishes glide rapidly through the upper atmosphere, which seemed to be a combination of heaven and ocean. Near the Seine, the course of which was altered, I came across a crowd of men clad in short blouses knotted at the waist, and wearing long gaiters. To all appearance they were in their working clothes. But their gait was

lighter and more elegant than that of our workmen. I noticed women among them. What had
heretofore prevented my recognising them as such
was that they were dressed like the men, that they
had long and straight legs, and, so it seemed to me,
the narrow hips of American women. Although
these folk did not present a savage appearance, I
looked at them with fright. They presented to my
gaze a more foreign appearance than any of the
numerous strangers I had so far met upon the earth.
In order to avoid seeing another human face, I
turned down a deserted lane. Very soon I came to
a circus planted with masts from which flew crimson oriflammes bearing in letters of gold the words:
EUROPEAN FEDERATION. Placards in large frames
ornamented with emblems of peace hung at the foot
of the masts. They embodied announcements regarding popular festivals, legal injunctions, and
works of public interest. In addition to balloon
time-tables was a chart of the atmospheric currents
drawn on the 28th of June of the year 220 of the
Federation of Nations. All these texts were printed
in characters new to me, and in a language of which
I did not understand all the words. The while I
was attempting to decipher them, the shadows of
the countless machines cleaving the air flitted across
my vision. Once more did I gaze upwards, and in
this sky altered beyond recognition, more densely
populated than the earth, cloven by rudders and

threshed by screws, towards which a circle of smoke rose from the horizon, I perceived the sun. I felt like crying on seeing it. It was the only familiar figure which I had come across since morning. From its altitude I judged that it was about ten o'clock of the forenoon. Of a sudden I was surrounded by a second crowd of men and women, similar in appearance and in costume to the first. I was confirmed in the impression that the women, although some of them were very plump, others very skinny, and many beggared description, were on the whole androginous in appearance. The crowd went its way. The open space once more was desert, just as our suburban quarters, which only come to life on the exodus from the workshops. I remained behind in front of the placards and read once more the date—the 28th of June of the year 220 of the European Federation. What did it mean! A proclamation by the Federal Committee, on the occasion of the festival of the Earth, furnished me with timely and useful data for comprehension of that date. This is what I read: 'Comrades, you are aware how, in the last years of the twentieth century, the old order collapsed in a fearful cataclysm, and how, after fifty years of anarchy, the federation of the peoples of Europe was organised. . . .' The year 220 of the federation of peoples was therefore the year 2270 of the Christian Era; this was certainly a fact which remained to be explained. How came it that of a sudden I found myself transported to the year 2270?

"I mused over the circumstances as I strolled at haphazard.

" 'I have not, as far as I know,' I said to myself, 'been preserved for so many years in the mummy state, like Colonel Fougas. I have not driven the machine with which Mr. H. G. Wells explores time. And if, following the example of William Morris, I have, while asleep, skipped three and a half centuries, I am unaware of the fact, since, when dreaming, one does not know that one is doing so. I am utterly convinced that I am not asleep.'

"While indulging in these musings and others not worth recording I was following a long street bordered with railings behind which pink-hued houses of various styles, but all equally small, smilingly peeped through the foliage. At times I perceived huge circuses of steel standing out in the landscape, and crowned with flames and smoke. Terror planed over these regions to which no name can be given, while the vibrating rush of air caused by the rapid flight of the machines resounded painfully through my brain. The street led to a meadow studded with clumps of trees and intersected by rivulets. Cows were pasturing in it. Just as my eyes were feasting upon the freshness of the scene I fancied I saw in front of me shadows flitting

along a smooth and straight road. The whirlwind
engendered by them, as they passed me, fanned my
cheeks. I saw that they were trams and automobiles, real transparencies in their rapidity.

"I crossed the road by a foot-bridge, and for a
long time I sauntered through small meadows and
woodlands. I thought I was in the open country,
when I discovered an extensive frontage of re-
splendent houses bordering on the park. Soon, I
found myself opposite a palace of an airy style of
architecture. A sculptured and painted frieze, rep-
resenting a largely attended feast, stretched across
the vast façade. I perceived, through the panes of
the bay-windows, men and women seated in a large
and bright room around long marble tables, laden
with prettily painted potteries. I entered, under the
impression that this was a restaurant. I was not
hungry, but weary, and the coolness of the room,
artistically hung with garlands of fruit, appeared to
me delicious. A man who stood by the door asked
me for my voucher, and, as I showed embarrassment,
he remarked:

" 'I see, comrade, that you are not of these parts.
How is it that you are travelling without vouchers!
Very sorry, but it is impossible for me to admit you.
Go and seek the delegate who hires journeymen; or,
if you are too weak to work, address yourself to the
delegate who attends to those who need succour.'

"I informed him that I was nowise unfit for work,

and drew away. A stout fellow, who was picking his teeth, said to me obligingly:

" 'Comrade, you need not go to the delegate who engages journeymen. I am the delegate attached to the bakery of the section. We are one comrade short. Come along with me. You shall be put to work at once.'

"I thanked the corpulent comrade, assured him of my willingness, pointing out, however, that I was not a baker.

"He looked at me with some surprise, and told me that he could see I enjoyed a joke.

"I followed him. We stopped in front of an immense cast-iron building having a monumental gateway, on the pediment of which a couple of bronze giants were resting on their elbows—the Sower and the Reaper. Their bodies expressed strength unstrained. A calm pride irradiated their faces, and they carried high their heads; in this, greatly dissimilar to the fierce-looking workers of the Flemish Constantin Meunier. We entered a room forty mètres in height, wherein, amid clouds of a light whitish dust, machinery was working with a sonorous and calm hum. Under the metallic dome, bags tendered themselves spontaneously to the knife which disembowelled them; the flour which escaped from them dropped into troughs where powerful hands of steel kneaded it into dough which flowed into moulds, which when full hastened to put themselves of their own accord into an oven as capacious and deep as a tunnel. Five or six men at most, motionless amid all this motion, supervised the labour of the machinery.

" ' 'Tis an old bakery,' said my companion. 'It hardly produces more than eighty thousand loaves a day, and its too weak machines employ too many hands. It matters little. Come up to the place where the goods arrive.'

"I did not have the time to ask for a more explicit command. A lift had deposited me on the platform. Hardly had I reached it, when a kind of flying whale alighted close to me and unloaded a number of sacks. No human being was aboard this machine. Other flying whales brought more sacks which they unloaded, and which offered themselves up in succession to the knife which ripped them open. The screws revolved, and the rudder did its work. There was no one at the helm, nobody aboard the machine. I could hear in the distance the slight hum of a wasp flying, and then the thing grew with astounding rapidity. It seemed quite sure of itself, but my ignorance as to what would happen, should it perchance go wrong, caused me to shudder. I was several times tempted to ask to be allowed to go down again. A false shame prevented me. I stood my ground. The sun was disappearing on the horizon, and it was about five o'clock when the lift came up for me. The day's work was over.   I was given a voucher for board and lodging.

"The rotund comrade remarked to me:

" 'You must be hungry.   'You may, if you wish, take your evening meal at the public table.   If you prefer eating by yourself in your own room, you may likewise do so.   If you prefer supping at my place, together with a few comrades, say so at once.   I am going to telephone to the culinary workshop that your rations be sent to you.   I am telling you all this in order to set you at ease, for you seem like a fish out of water.   You have no doubt come from afar.   You do not look as if you could take care of yourself.   To-day, your task has been an easy one.   Do not, however, imagine that one's livelihood is earned every day as cheaply as that.   If the Z-rays which directed the balloons had worked badly, as will sometimes happen, your task would not have been so easy.   What is your particular line, and where do you come from?'

"These questions embarrassed me greatly.   I could not tell him the truth.   I could not inform him that I was a bourgeois, and that I had come from the twentieth century.   He would have thought me crazy.   I replied in a vague and embarrassed manner that I had no trade, and that I came from far, from very far.

"He smiled, and said:

" 'I understand.   You dare not admit it.   You

come from the United States of Africa. You are not the only European who has thus given us the slip. But nearly all these deserters end by coming back to us.'

"I answered not a word, and my silence led him to believe that he had guessed aright. He renewed his invitation to supper, and asked me my name. I informed him that I was known as Hippolyte Dufresne. He seemed surprised at my having two names.

" 'My name is Michel,' he said.

"Then, after a minute inspection of my straw hat, my jacket, my shoes, and the rest of my costume, which was no doubt somewhat dusty, but of a good cut, for after all I do not have my clothes made by a tailor who acts as hall-porter in the Rue de Acacias, he continued:

" 'Hippolyte, I see whence you have come. You have lived in the black provinces. Nowadays there are only Zulus and Basutos to weave cloth so badly, to give so grotesque a shape to a suit, to make such ill-shapen footgear, and to stiffen linen with starch. It is only among them that you can have learnt to shave off your beard, while preserving on your face a moustache, and two little whiskers. This custom of scissoring the hair of the face, so as to form figures and ornaments, is the last word of tattooing, nowadays in vogue only among the Basutos and Zulus. These black provinces of the United States of Africa are wallowing in a state of barbarism resembling in many aspects the state of France three or four hundred years ago.'

"I accepted Michel's invitation.

" 'I live quite close to here, in Sologne,' he said. 'My aeroplane scuds along fairly well. We shall soon be there.'

"He made me take a seat under the belly of a huge mechanical bird, and we were soon cleaving the air so rapidly that I lost breath. The aspect of the countryside was vastly different from the one known to me. All the roads were bordered with houses; countless canals intersected the fields with their silvery lines. As I sat wrapt in admiration, Michel remarked to me:

" 'The land is fairly well exploited, and cultivation is "intense," as they say, since chemists are themselves agriculturists. One has tried one's best, and one has worked hard for the past three hundred years. The fact is that to make collectivism a reality it has been necessary to compel the soil to return four or five times more than it returned in the days of capitalistic anarchy. You, who have lived among the Zulus and Basutos, are aware that the necessaries of life are so scarce with them that were they to be divided among all it would amount to sharing poverty and not wealth. The superabundant production which we have attained to is more especially due to the progress made by science.

The almost total suppression of the urban classes
has also been of great advantage to agriculture.
The shopkeepers and the clerks have gone, some to
the factory, others to the field.'

" 'What!' I exclaimed. 'You have suppressed
the cities! What has become of Paris?'

" 'Hardly any one lives there now,' replied Michel. 'The greater part of those hideous and in-
sanitary five-storied houses, wherein dwelt the citizens of the closed era, have fallen in ruins, and
have been suffered to remain in that condition.
House-building was very poor in the twentieth century of that unhappy era. We have preserved
some of the older and better constructed buildings
and converted them into museums. We possess a
large number of museums and libraries: it is there
we seek instruction. We have also kept a portion
of the remains of the Hôtel de Ville. It was an ugly
and fragile building, but great things were carried
out within its precincts. As we no longer have
tribunals, commerce, and armies, we no longer have
cities, so to speak. Nevertheless, the density of the
population is much greater on certain points than
on others, and in spite of the rapidity of means of
communication, the mining and metallurgic centres
are densely peopled.'

" 'What is that you say?' I asked him. 'You
have done away with the courts of law? Have you
then suppressed crime and misdemeanour?'

" 'Crime will last as long as old and gloomy humanity. But, the number of criminals has diminished with the number of the wretched. The suburbs of the great cities were the feeding-grounds of crime; we no longer have big cities. The wireless telephone makes the highways safe day and night. We are all provided with electric means of defence. As to misdemeanors, they were rather the result of the scruples of the judges than of the perversity of the accused. Now that we no longer possess lawyers and judges, and that justice is administered by citizens summoned in rotation, many misdemeanours have disappeared, doubtless because it is impossible to recognise them as such.'

"In this fashion did Michel discourse while steering his aeroplane. I am recording the meaning of his words as exactly as I can. I regret my inability, owing to a lack of memory, and also from fear of not making myself understood, to reproduce his language in all its expressiveness and its movement. The baker and his contemporaries spoke a language astonishing me at first by the novelty of its vocabulary and syntax, and especially by its pithy and flowing construction.

"Michel came to ground on the terrace of a modest but pleasing dwelling.

" 'We have arrived,' he said; ' 'tis here that I live. You will sup with comrades who, like myself, take an interest in statistics.'

" 'What! You a statistician! I thought you were a baker.

" 'I am a baker, six hours of the day. This is the duration of the day's work as determined for nearly a century by the Federal Committee. The rest of the time I give up to statistical labours. It is the science which has stepped into history's shoes. The historians of old related the brilliant deeds of the few. Ours register all that is produced and consumed.'

"After having conducted me to a hydrotherapic closet established on the roof, Michel led me downstairs to the dining-room lit up by electricity, entirely white, and ornamented only with a sculptured frieze of strawberry plants in bloom. A table in painted pottery was covered with dishes with a metallic glaze. Three persons sat at it. Michel named them to me.

" 'Morin, Perceval, Cheron.'

These three individuals were all clad alike in rough-spun jackets, velvet breeches, and grey stockings. Morin wore a long white beard; Chéron's and Perceval's faces were callow. Their short hair and more especially the frankness of their looks gave them the appearance of young lads. Yet I felt sure that they were women. Percival seemed to me rather pretty, although she was no longer very young. I thought Chéron altogether charming. Michel introduced me:

" 'I have brought comrade Hippolyte, who also calls himself Dufresne, to meet you; he has lived among the half-breeds, in the black provinces of the United States of Africa. He could not get any dinner at eleven o'clock, and so he must have an appetite.'

"I was indeed hungry. They helped me to tiny bits of food cut into squares, which were not unpleasant to the taste, however new to me. A variety of cheeses were on the table. Morin poured me out a glass of light beer, and informed me that I could drink to my heart's content, as it did not contain any alcohol.

" 'That's right,' I said. 'I am glad to see that you pay attention to the evils of alcohol.'

" 'They have almost ceased to exist,' answered Morin. 'We succeeded in suppressing alcoholism before the end of the closed era. It would have otherwise been impossible to establish the new *régime*. An alcoholic proletariat is incapable of emancipation.

" 'Have you not also,' I inquired, while tasting a strangely carved bit of food—'have you not also perfected food?'

" 'Comrade,' replied Perceval, 'you doubtless refer to chemical alimentation. So far, it has not made any great strides. 'Tis in vain that we send our chemists as delegates into the kitchen. . . . Their tabloids are of no good. With the exception

that we know how to compound properly caloric
and nutritious foods, we feed almost as coarsely as
the men of the closed era, and we enjoy it just
as much.'

" 'Our scientists,' remarked Michel, 'are seeking
to establish a rational system of food.'

" 'That's childishness,' said the young female
Chéron. 'No good result will be reached, as long
as the big intestine, a useless and harmful organ,
and the seat of microbian infection, has not been
removed. . . . This will come in time.'

" 'In what way?' I asked.

" 'Simply by ablation. And this suppression, the
result, in the first place, of an operation upon a
sufficient number of individuals, will tend to establish
itself by heredity, and will later on be common to
the whole race.'

"These people treated me humanely and con-
versed obligingly with me. But it was difficult for
me to chime in with their manners and their ideas,
while I noticed that I nowise interested them, and
that they felt an absolute indifference towards my
modes of thought. The more I showed them cour-
tesies, the more I alienated their sympathies. Following upon my addressing a few compliments, al-
beit discreet and sincere, to Chéron, she no longer
even deigned to look at me.

"The meal over, addressing myself to Morin,
who seemed to me intelligent and gentle, I said to

him with a sincerity which indeed stirred me deeply:

" 'Monsieur Morin, I am ignorant of all things, and I am suffering cruelly because of my lack of knowledge. I repeat to you that I come from far, from very far. Tell me, I entreat you, how the European Federation came into existence, and explain to me the present social system.'

"Old Morin protested:

" 'You are asking me for the history of three centuries. It would take me weeks, nay months. Moreover, there are many things I could not teach you, as I do not know them myself.'

"I thereupon entreated him to lay before me a very concise summary, as is done in the case of school children.

"Morin, flinging himself back in his arm-chair, began:

" 'To ascertain how the present society was constituted, it is necessary to go back far into the past.

" 'The crowning achievement of the twentieth century was the extinction of war.

" 'The arbitration Congress of The Hague, instituted in the middle of barbarism, did not to any degree contribute towards the maintenance of peace. But another more efficacious institution came into existence at that time. Groups of deputies were formed in the various Parliaments, who entered into communication with one another, and who in course

of time came to deliberate in common on international questions. Giving expression as they did
to the peaceful aspirations of a growing crowd of
electors, their resolutions carried great weight, and
supplied food for reflection to the governments, the
most absolute of which, if one sets aside Russia, had
at that time learnt to reckon with popular sentiment. What surprises us nowadays is that no
one discerned in those meetings of deputies come
together from all countries the first attempt at an
international parliament.

" 'But then the party of violence was still powerful in the several empires, and even in the French
Republic. And if the danger of the old-time dy-
nastic and diplomatic wars determined upon at a
green-baized table for the purpose of maintaining
what was known as the European equilibrium was
averted for all time, it was still to be dreaded, considering the unsatisfactory industrial condition affecting Europe, that the conflicting industrial interests might bring about some terrible conflagration.

" 'The imperfectly organised proletariat, as yet
without the consciousness of its strength, did not
put an end to armed struggles between nations,
but it limited their frequency and duration.

" 'The last wars were the outcome of that mad
fury of the old world known as the colonial policy.
English, Russians, Germans, French, and Americans

joined in rabid competition, in Asia and Africa, for the possession of zones of influence, as they said, wherein they could, on the basis of pillage and massacres, establish economic relations with the aborigines. They destroyed everything they could destroy in those two countries. Then followed the inevitable. The impoverished colonies which were expensive were retained and the prosperous ones lost. But mankind had to reckon, in Asia, with a small heroic nation, taught by Europe, which made itself respected by her. By so doing, Japan, in barbarous times, rendered a great service to humanity.

" 'When at last that detestable period of colonisation came to an end, no further was there any war. Still the States continued keeping up armies.

" 'Having so far explained matters, I shall proceed to lay before you, pursuant to your request, the origins of present-day society. It issued from the one preceding it. In moral just as in individual life forms generate one another. Capitalistic naturally enough produced collectivist society. At the commencement of the twentieth century of the closed era, a memorable industrial evolution took place. The slender production of small artisans whose all were their tools was followed by a great production financially supported by a new agent of marvellous power—capital. Here was a great social progress.'

" 'What was a great social step in advance?' I asked.

" 'The capitalistic *régime*,' replied Morin. 'It brought humanity an untold source of wealth. By grouping the workers in considerable masses and multiplying their numbers it created the proletariat. By making the workers an immense State within the State it paved the way for their emancipation, and furnished them with the means of conquering power.

" 'This *régime*, however, which was to be productive of such happy results in the future, was execrated by the workers, in whose ranks it made countless victims.

" 'There exists no social benefit which has not been purchased at the cost of blood and tears. Moreover, this *régime* which had enriched the whole world came within an ace of ruining it. After having increased production to a considerable extent, it failed in its endeavours to regulate it, and struggled hopelessly in the toils of inextricable difficulties.

" 'You are not totally ignorant, comrade, of the economic disturbances which filled the twentieth century. During the last hundred years of the capitalistic domination, the disorder of production and the delirium of competition piled up disasters high. The capitalists and the masters vainly attempted, by means of gigantic combinations, to regulate production and to annihilate competition. Their ill-conceived undertakings were engulfed in an abyss of gigantic catastrophes. During those anarchical days, the fight between classes was blind and terrible. The proletariat, overwhelmed in the same ratio by its victories and its defeats, overwhelmed by the ruins of the edifice which it was pulling down on its own head, torn by fearful internal struggles, casting aside in its blind violence its best leaders and most trustworthy friends, fought on without system and in the dark. It was, however, continually winning some advantage: an increase of wages, shorter hours of work, a growing freedom of organisation and of propaganda, the conquest of public power, and making progress in the dumfounded public mind. It was looked upon as wrecked through its divisions and mistakes. But all great parties are at odds, and all commit blunders. The proletariat had on its side the force of events. Towards the end of the century it attained the degree of well-being which opens the way to better things. Comrade, a party must have within itself a certain strength in order to accomplish a revolution favourable to its interests. Towards the end of the twentieth century of the closed era the general situation had become most favourable to the developments of socialism. The standing armies, more and more reduced during the course of the century, were abolished, following upon a desperate opposition of the powers that were, and of the bourgeosie owning all things, by Chambers born of universal suffrage under the fiery pressure of the people of the cities and of the country. For a long time past already, the chiefs of State had retained their armies, less in view of a war which they no longer dreaded or could hope for, than to hold in check the multitude of proletaries at home. In the end, they yielded. Militias imbued with socialistic ideas supplanted regular armies. It was not without good cause that the governments showed opposition. No longer defended by guns and rifles, the monarchical systems succumbed in succession, and Republican Government stepped into their places. Alone, England, who had previously established a *régime* considered endurable by the workers, and Russia, who had remained Imperialist and theocratic, stood outside the pale of this great movement. It was feared that the Czar, who felt towards republican Europe the sentiments which the French Revolution had inspired the great Catherine with, might raise armies to combat it. But his government had reached a degree of weakness and imbecility which only an absolute monarchy can attain. The Russian proletariat, joining hands with the intellectuals, rose in revolt, and after an awful succession of outrages and massacres, power passed into the hands of the revolutionaries, who established the representative system.

" 'Telegraphy and wireless telephony were then
in use from one end of Europe to the other, and so
easy of use that the poorest of individuals could
speak, whenever he wished, and give utterance to
whatever he saw fit to a fellow creature living in
any corner of the globe. Collectivist ideas rained
down on Moscow. The Russian peasants could
listen in their beds to the speeches of their comrades
of Marseilles and Berlin. Simultaneously, the ap-
proximate steering of balloons and the exact course
of flying-machines came into practical use. The
result was the abolition of frontiers. This was the
most critical moment of all. The patriotic instinct
took a fresh life in the hearts of the nations so near
uniting and fusing into one boundless humanity. In
all countries, and at one and the same time, the
nationalist faith, rekindled, emitted flashes of light.
As there were no longer any kings, armies, or aristocracy, this great movement assumed a tumultuous
and popular character. The French Republic, the
German Republic, the Hungarian Republic, the
Roman Republic, the Italian Republic, and even the
Swiss and Belgian Republics, each expressed by a
unanimous vote of their respective Parliaments, and
at largely attended meetings, the solemn resolve to
defend against all foreign aggression national territory and industry. Stringent laws were promulgated
repressing the smuggling by flying-machines, and
regulating severely the use of wireless telegraphy.

The militia was everywhere reorganised and brought back to the old type of standing armies. Once more did the former uniforms, boots, dolmans, and generals' plumes make their appearance. Fur busbies were anew welcomed with the applause of Paris. All the shopkeepers and a portion of the workmen donned the tricolour cockade. In all foundry districts, cannon and armour-plates were once more forged. Terrible wars were anticipated. This mad spurt lasted three years, without matters coming to a clash, and then it slackened imperceptibly. The militias gradually recovered the bourgeois aspect and feeling. The union of nations, which had seemed postponed to a fabled remoteness, was near at hand. Pacific efforts were developing day by day; collectivists were gradually achieving the conquest of society. The day came at last when the defeated capitalists abandoned the field to them.'

" 'What a change!' I exclaimed. 'History cannot show another example of such a revolution.'

" 'You may well imagine, comrade,' resumed Morin, 'that collectivism did not make its appearance till the appointed hour. The Socialists could not have suppressed capital and individual property had not those two forms of wealth been already all but destroyed *de facto* by the efforts of the proletariat, and still more so by the fresh developments of science and industry.

" 'It had indeed been thought that Germany would

be the first collectivist State; the Labour Party had there been organized for about one hundred years, and it was everywhere said: "Socialism is a thing German?" Still, France, less well prepared, got the start of her. The social revolution broke out in the first place at Lyons, Lille, and Marseilles, to the strains of *l'Internationale*. Paris held aloof for a fortnight, and then hoisted the red flag. It was only on the following day that Berlin proclaimed the collectivist state. The triumph of socialism had as a result the union of nations.

" 'The delegates of all the European Republics, sitting in Brussels, proclaimed the Constitution of the United States of Europe.

" 'England refused to form part of it, but she declared herself its ally. While having become socialistic, she had retained her king, her lords, and even the wigs of her judges. Socialism was at that time supreme ruler in Oceanic, China, Japan, and in a portion of the vast Russian Republic. Black Africa, which had entered upon the capitalistic phase, formed a confederation of little homogeneity. The American Union had a while ago renounced mercantile militarism. The condition of the world was consequently favourable, upon the whole, to the free development of the United States of Europe. Nevertheless, this union, welcomed with delirious joy, was followed for the space of half a century by economic disturbances and social miseries. There were no longer any armies, and hardly any militias; in consequence of not being constricted, popular movements did not take the form of violent outbreaks. But the inexperience or the ill-will of the local governments was fostering a ruinous state of disorder.

" 'Fifty years after the constitution of the States, the disappointments were so cruel, and the difficulties seemed to such a degree insurmountable, that the most optimistic spirits were beginning to despair. Smothered crackings foretold in all directions the dismemberment of the Union. It was then that the dictatorship of a committee composed of fourteen workmen put an end to anarchy, and organised the Federation of European nations as it exists to-day. There are those who say that the Fourteen displayed unparalleled genius and relentless energy; others claim that they were mediocrities terrified and influenced by the stress of necessity, and that they presided as if in spite of themselves over the spontaneous organisation of the new social forces. It is at all events certain that they did not go against the tide of events. The organisation which they established, or witnessed the establishment of, still subsists almost in its entirety. The production and consumption of goods are nowadays carried out, to all purposes, according to the rules laid down in those days. The new era justly dates from that time.'

"Morin then expounded to me most succinctly the principles of modern society.

" 'It rests,' said he, 'on the total suppression of individual property.'

" 'Is not this intolerable to you?' I asked.

" 'Why should we find it unendurable, Hippolyte? In Europe, formerly, the State collected the taxes. It disposed of resources proper to it. Nowadays it can be said with an equal degree of truth that it possesses everything, while possessing nothing. It is still more exact to say that it is we who own all things, since the State is not a thing apart from us, and is merely the expression of collectiveness.'

" 'But,' I asked, 'do you not possess anything proper to yourself? Not even the plates out of which you eat, nor your bed, your bed-sheets, your clothes?'

"Morin smiled at my question.

" 'You are a deal more simple than I dreamt, Hippolyte. What! You imagine that we are not the owners of our personal property. What can well be your idea of our taste, our instincts, our needs, and our mode of living? Do you take us for monks, as was said in olden days, for men destitute of all individual character and incapable of affixing a personal impress on our surroundings? You are mistaken, my friend, altogether mistaken. We hold as our own the objects destined to our use

and comfort, and we feel more attached to them
than were the bourgeois of the closed era to their
knick-knacks, for our taste is keener, and we possess
a livelier sentiment of form. All our comrades of
some refinement own works of art, and take great
pride in them. Chéron has in her home paintings
which are her delight, and she would take it amiss
were the Federal Committee to contest with her the
possession of them. Personally, I preserve in that
closet some ancient drawings, the almost complete
work of Steinlen, one of the most highly prized
artists of the closed era. Neither silver nor gold
would tempt me to part with them.

" 'Whence have you come, Hippolyte? You
are told that our society is based on the total suppression of individual property, and you get into
your head that such suppression covers goods and
chattels, and articles in daily use. But, you simple-
minded fellow, the individual property totally suppressed by us is the ownership of the means of production, soil, canals, roads, mines, material, plant,
&c. It does not affect lamps and arm-chairs.
What we have done away with is the possibility of
diverting to the benefit of an individual or of a
group of individuals the fruits of labour; 'tis not
the natural and harmless possession of the beloved
chattels about us.'

"Morin next enlightened me as to the distribution of intellectual and manual labours among all the members of the community, in conformity with their aptitudes.

" 'Collectivist society,' he went on to say, 'differs not only from capitalistic society in the fact that in the former everybody works. During the closed era, the people who toiled not were in great numbers; still, they constituted the minority. Our society differs more especially from the former in that labour was not properly classified, and that many useless tasks were performed. The workers produced without systematic order, method, and concerted action. The cities were full of officials, magistrates, merchants, and clerks, who worked without producing. There were also the soldiers. The fruits of labour were not properly distributed. The customs and tariffs established for the purpose of remedying the evil merely aggravated matters. All were suffering. Production and consumption are now minutely regulated. Lastly, our society differs from the old one in that we enjoy all the benefits derived from machinery, the use of which, in the capitalistic age, was so frequently disastrous for the workers.'

"I asked him how it had been possible to constitute a society composed wholly of workmen.

"Morin pointed out to me that man's aptitude for work is general, and that it constitutes one of the essential characteristics of the race.

" 'In barbarian times,' he said, 'and right until the end of the closed era, the aristocratic and wealthy classes always showed a preference for manual labour. They put their intellectual faculties to an infinitesimal use, and in exceptional instances at that. Their tastes always inclined towards such occupations as the chase and war, wherein the body plays a greater part than the mind. They rode, drove, fenced, and practised pistol-shooting. It may therefore be said of them that they worked with their hands. Their work was either sterile or harmful, for the reason that a certain prejudice forbade them to engage in any useful or beneficent work, and also, because in their day, useful work was most often carried out under ignoble and disgusting conditions. It did not prove so very difficult to impart a taste for work to every one by reinstating it in a position of honour. The men of the barbaric ages took pride in carrying a gun or wearing a sword. The men of to-day are proud of handling a spade or a hammer. Humanity rests on a foundation which undergoes but little change.'

"Morin having told me that the very memory of all monetary circulation had become lost, I asked him:

" 'How then do you carry on business without cash payments?'

" 'We exchange products by means of vouchers similar to those just given you, comrade, and they correspond to the hours of labour performed by us. The value of the products is computed by the length of time their production has taken. Bread, meat, beer, clothes, an aeroplane, represent x hours, x days of labour. From each of these vouchers, collectivism, or as it was styled formerly, the State, deducts a certain number of minutes for the purpose of allocating them to unproductive works, metallurgic and alimentary reserves, refuges and private asylums, and so forth.'

" 'These minutes,' interjected Michel, 'are continually increasing apace. The Federal Committee orders far too many great works, the burden of which is thus on our shoulders. The reserve stocks are far too considerable. The public warehouses are crowded to overflowing with riches of all sorts. 'Tis our minutes of labour which are entombed there. Many abuses are still in existence.'

" 'No doubt,' replied Morin, 'there is room for improvement. The wealth of Europe, which has accrued through general methodical labour, is untold.'

"I was curious to learn whether these folk had no other measurement of labour than the time required for its accomplishment, and whether in their case the day's work of the navvy or of the journeyman tempering plaster ranked with that of the chemist or the surgeon. I put the question frankly.

" 'What a silly question,' exclaimed Perceval.

"Nevertheless old Morin vouchsafed to enlighten me.

" 'All works of study, of research, in fact all works contributing to render life better and more beautiful are encouraged in our workshops and laboratories. The collectivist State fosters the higher studies. To study is akin to producing, since nothing is produced without study. Study, just as much as work, entitles one to existence. Those who devote themselves to long and arduous research secure unto themselves a peaceful and respected existence. It takes a sculptor a fortnight to make the *maquette* of a figure, but he has worked five years to learn modelling. Now the State has paid him for his maquette during those five years. A chemist discovers in a few hours the particular properties of a body. But he has spent months in isolating this body, and years in fitting himself to become capable of such an undertaking. During the whole of that time he has lived at the expense of the State. A surgeon removes a tumour in ten minutes. This is the result of fifteen years of study and practice. He has, as a consequence, received vouchers from the State for fifteen years past. Every man who gives in a month, in an hour, in a few minutes, the product of his whole life, is merely repaying in a lump sum what collectivism has given him day by day.'

" 'Without reckoning,' said Percival, 'that our

great intellectuals, our surgeons, our lady doctors, our chemists, know full well how to derive profit from their works and discoveries, and to add beyond measure to their enjoyments. They cause to be allotted to themselves aerial machines of 60 h. p., palaces, gardens, and immense parks. They are, for the greater part, individuals keenly alive to laying hold of the world's goods, and lead a more splendid and more copious existence than the bourgeois of the closed era. The worst of it is that the majority of them are stupid fools who should be recruited for work at the flour-mills, like Hippolyte.'

"I bowed my thanks. Michel approved Percival, and bitterly lamented the accommodating mind of the State in its system of fattening chemists at the expense of the workers.

"I asked whether the negotiation of the vouchers did not bring about a rise and fall.

" 'Speculation in vouchers,' replied Morin, 'is prohibited. As a matter of fact, it cannot be prevented altogether. There are among us, just as formerly, avaricious and prodigal, laborious and idle, rich and poor, happy and miserable, contented and discontented men. Yet all manage to exist, and that is already something.'

"I fell a-musing for a while; then I remarked:

" 'Monsieur Morin, if one is to believe you, it

seems to me that you have realised equality and
fraternity, as much as possible. But I fear that it
is at the expense of liberty, which I have learnt to
cherish as the best of things.'

"Morin shrugged his shoulders, saying:

" 'We have not established equality. We know
what it means. We have secured a livelihood for
all. We have placed labour on a pedestal of
honour. After that, if the bricklayer thinks himself superior to the poet, and the poet to the
bricklayer, 'tis their business. Every one of our
workers imagines that his form of labour is the
grandest in the world. The advantages of this idea
are greater than the disadvantages.

" 'Comrade Hippolyte, you seem to have delved
deeply into the books of the nineteenth century of the
closed era; their leaves are hardly turned nowadays:
you speak their language, to us a foreign tongue.
It is hard for us to realise nowadays that the bygone
friends of the people should have adopted as their
motto: *Liberty, Equality, Fraternity.* Liberty has
no place in society, since it does not exist in nature.
There is no free animal. It was said formerly that
a man who obeyed the laws was free. This was
childish. Moreover, so strange a use was made of
the word liberty in the last days of the capitalistic
anarchy that the word has ended in merely expressing the setting claim to privileges. The idea
of equality is still less reasonable, and it is an

unfortunate idea in that it presupposes a false ideal. We have not to seek whether men are equal among themselves. What we must see to is that each one shall supply his best and receive all necessaries of life. As to fraternity, we know only too well how brothers have acted towards brothers during the course of centuries. We do not pretend to say that men are bad. We do not say that they are good. They are what they are, but they live in peace, when there are no longer any reasons for them to fight one another. We have but a single word to express our social system. We say that we live in harmony. Now it is an assured fact that all human forces act in concert nowadays.'

" 'In the centuries,' I said to him, 'of what you styled the closed era, one preferred the possession of things to their enjoyment. I can conceive that, reversing the order of things, you prefer enjoyment to possession. But is it not distressing to you not to have any property to leave to your children?'

" 'In capitalistic times,' replied Morin with animation, 'how many were there who left inheritances? One in a thousand; nay, one in ten thousand. Nor must it be forgotten that many generations did not enjoy the faculty of bequeathing. Be this as it may, the transmission of fortune through the medium of inheritances was perfectly conceivable when the family was in existence. But now . . .'

" 'What!' I exclaimed, 'you have no family ties?'

"My surprise, which I had not been able to conceal, seemed comical to the woman-comrade Chéron.

" 'We are quite aware,' she said to me, 'that marriage exists among the Kaffirs. We European women do not bind ourselves by promises; or, if we make them, the law does not take cognisance of them. We are of opinion that the whole destiny of a human being should not hang on a word. Nevertheless, there survives a relic of the customs of the closed era. When a woman gives herself, she swears fidelity on the horns of the moon. In reality, neither the man nor the woman takes any binding engagement. Yet it is not of rare occurrence that their union endures as long as life. Neither of them would wish to be the object of a fidelity secured by means of an oath, instead of by physical and moral expediency. We owe nothing to anybody. Formerly, a man convinced a woman that she belonged to him. We are less simple-minded. We believe that a human being belongs to itself alone. We give ourselves when we please, and to whom we see fit.

" 'Moreover, we feel no shame in yielding to

desire. We are no hypocrites. Only four hundred years ago physiology was a sealed book to men, and their ignorance was the cause of dire illusions and cruel deceptions. Hippolyte, whatever the Kaffirs may say, society must be subordinate to nature, and not, as too long has been the case, nature to society?'

"Perceval, endorsing the speech of her comrade, added:

" 'To show you how the sex question is regulated in our society, I must tell you, Hippolyte, that in many factories the recruiting delegate does not even inquire about one's sex. The sex of an individual does not interest collectivism."

" 'But the children?'

" 'Well? The children?'

" 'Not having any family ideal, are they not neglected?'

" 'Whence did you get such an idea? Maternal love is a most powerful instinct in woman. In the hideous society of the past, mothers were to be seen courting misery and shame, in order to bring up illegitimate offspring. Why should ours, exempt as they are from shame and misery, forsake their little ones? There are among us many good partners, and many good mothers. But there is a very large number, which increases apace, of women who dispense with men.'

"Chéron made in this connection a somewhat strange remark.

" 'We have in regard to sexual characteristics,' she said, 'notions undreamt of in the barbaric simplicity of the men of the closed era. False conclusions were for a long time drawn from the fact that there are two sexes, and two only. It was therefrom concluded that a woman is absolutely female, and a man absolutely male. In reality, it is not thus; there are women who are very much women, while others are very little so. These differences, formerly concealed by the costume and the mode of life and disguised by prejudice, make themselves clearly manifest in our society. More than that, they become accentuated and more marked with each succeeding generation. Ever since women have worked like men, and acted and thought like them, many are to be found who resemble men. We may some day reach the point of creating neutrals, and produce female workers, as in the case of bees. It will prove a great benefit, for it will become possible to increase the quantity of work without increasing the population in a degree out of proportion to the necessaries of life. We entertain the same dread of a deficit in and a surplus of births.'

"I thanked Perceval and Chéron for having kindly supplied me with information on so interesting a subject, and I inquired whether education was not neglected in collectivist society, and whether speculative science and the liberal arts still flourished.

"The following is old Morin's reply to my question:

" 'Education, in all its degrees, is highly developed. The comrades all know something; they do not know the same things, nor have they learnt anything useless. No longer is any time lost in the study of law and theology. Each one selects from the arts and sciences what suits him. We still possess many ancient works, although the greater part of the works printed before the new era have perished. Books are still printed in greater quantity than ever. And yet typography is on the point of disappearing. Phonography will take its place. Poets and novelists are already being published phonographically, while in connection with theatrical plays, a most ingenious combination of the phono and the cinemato rendering both the voice and the play of the actors has been devised.'

" 'You have then poets and playwrights?'

" 'We not only have poets, but a poetry of our own. We are the first who have delimitated the domain of poetry. Previous to our time, many ideas which could have been better expressed in prose were expressed in verse. Narratives were unfolded in rhyme. This was a survival of the days when legislative enactments and recipes of rural economy were drawn up in measured terms. Nowadays poets merely sing delicate subjects which have no meaning, while their grammar and language are as proper to them as their rhythm and assonance. As to our stage, it is almost exclusively lyric. A precise knowledge of reality and a life void of violence have rendered us almost indifferent to drama and tragedy. The uniformity of the classes and the equality of the sexes have deprived the old comedy of nearly all its subject-matter. But never has music been so beautiful and so beloved. We especially admire the sonata and the symphony.

" 'Our society is greatly predisposed in favour of the arts of design. Many prejudices harmful to painting have vanished. Our life is more limpid and more beautiful than the bourgeois life, and we have a vivid appreciation of form. Sculpture is in a still more flourishing condition than painting, ever since it has taken an intelligent part in the ornamentation of public buildings and private dwellings. Never was so much done towards the teaching of art. If you will but steer your aeroplane above one of our streets, you will be surprised at the number of schools and museums.'

" 'To sum matters up, are you happy?' I inquired.

"Morin shook his head and replied:

" 'It is not in human nature to enjoy perfect happiness. Happiness is not attainable without effort, and every effort brings with it fatigue and suffering. We have made life endurable to all. That is something. Our descendants will do better still. Our organisation is not immutable. Not fifty years ago, it was different from what it is to-day. Men endowed with subtle powers of observation believe that we are on the road to great changes. That may be. However, the forward steps in human civilisation will henceforth be harmonious and pacific.'

" 'Do you not fear, on the contrary,' I asked him, 'that the civilisation with which you appear to be satisfied may be destroyed by an invasion of barbarians? There still remain in Asia and Africa, so you have told me, large black or yellow populations which have not entered into your concert. They have armies, while you have none. Were they to attack you . . .'

" 'Our defence is assured. The Americans and the Australians alone could enter upon a struggle with us, for they are as learned as ourselves. But the ocean separates us and a community of interests makes us sure of their amity. As to the capitalistic negroes, they have not got any further than the steel cannon, fire-arms and all the old scrap-iron of the twentieth century. What could these ancient engines of war do against a discharge of Y-rays? Our

frontiers are protected by electricity. A zone of
lightning encircles the Federation. A little spec-
tacled fellow is sitting I know not where, in front
of a key-board. He is our one and only soldier.
He has but to touch a key in order to reduce to
dust an army of 500,000 men.'

"Morin ceased speaking for a moment; then he
continued speaking more deliberately:

" 'Were our civilisation threatened, it would not
be by any outside enemy. It would be by the enemies from within.'

" 'There are such enemies, then?'

" 'We have the anarchists. They are many,
fiery, and intelligent. Our chemists and our professors of sciences and letters are almost to a man
anarchists. They attribute to the regulation of
labour and production the majority of the evils
which still afflict society. They argue that humanity will not be happy except in the spontaneous harmony to be born of the total destruction of civilisation. They are dangerous. They would be still
more so were we to repress them. To do this,
however, we have neither the means nor the desire.
We do not possess any power of coercion or repression, and we get along very well without it. In
the barbaric ages, men nurtured great illusions in
regard to the efficacy of penalties. Our fathers
suppressed the judiciary system entirely. They no
longer required it. With the suppression of private

property, they simultaneously suppressed theft and swindling. Ever since we have carried electric protectors, assaults are no longer to be feared. Man has come to be respected by man. Crimes of passion are still and will ever be committed. However, such crimes as these, if left unpunished, become rarer. Our entire judiciary body is composed of elected arbitrators who try gratuitously all offences and disputes.'

" 'I rose, and thanking my comrades for their kindness, I begged Morin the favour of putting one more question to him.

" 'You no longer have any religion?'

" 'Quite the contrary; we have a large number of religions, some of them somewhat novel. To mention France only, we have the religion of humanity, positivism, Christianity, and spiritualism. In some countries there are still some Catholics, but they are few and split up into sects, as the result of schisms which occurred in the twentieth century, when Church and State drifted apart. For a long time now there has not been any Pope.'

" 'You are mistaken,' said Michel. 'There is still a Pope. It is by a mere chance that I know of him. He is Pius XXV., dyer, Via dell' Orso, in Rome.'

" 'What!' I exclaimed, 'the Pope is a dyer!' "

" 'What is there surprising about that! He must perforce have a trade, just as everybody else.'

" 'But his Church?'

" 'He is recognised by a few thousands, in Europe.'

"With these words, we parted. Michel informed me that I should find a lodging in the neighbourhood, and that Chéron would conduct me to it on her way home.

"The night was illuminated with an opalescent light both powerful and soft. It gave the foliage the sheen of enamel. I walked by the side of Chéron.

"I looked her over. Her flat-soled shoes gave firmness to her gait and balance to her body; although her male habiliments made her seem smaller than she was, and in spite of her having one hand in her pocket, her perfectly simple carriage did not lack dignity. She gazed freely to the right and left of her. She was the first woman in whom I had noticed the air of a curious and amused lounger. Her features, seen from under her tam-o'-shanter, were refined and strongly defined. She both irritated and charmed me. I was in dread that she might consider me stupid and ridiculous. It was, to say the least, plain that my personality inspired her with supreme indifference. Nevertheless, of a sudden she asked me what my trade might be. I answered at haphazard that I was an electrician.

" 'So am I,' she said.

"I prudently put an end to the conversation.

"Unheard-of sounds were filling the night air with their calm rhythmic noise, and I listened in affright to the respiration of the monstrous genius of this new world.

"The more I looked at the female electrician, the more did I feel a desire for her, a desire fanned by a dash of antipathy.

" 'So of course,' I said to her of a sudden, 'you have regulated love scientifically, and 'tis a matter which no longer causes any one uneasiness.'

" 'You are mistaken,' she replied. 'We have naturally got beyond the mad imbecility of the closed era, and the whole domain of human physiology is henceforth freed from legal barbarisms and theological terrors. We are no longer the prey to an erroneous and cruel conception of duty. But the laws governing the attraction between body and body are still a mystery to us. The spirit of the species is what it ever was and ever shall be, violent and capricious. Now, just as formerly, instinct remains stronger than reason. Our superiority over the ancients lies less in the knowledge of it than in proclaiming it. We have within us a force capable of creating worlds, to wit, desire, and you would have us regulate it. 'Tis asking too much of us. We are no longer barbarians. We have not yet become wise. Collectivism altogether ignores all that appertains to sexual relations. These relations are what they may be, most often tolerable, rarely delicious, and at times horrible. But, comrade, do not imagine that love no longer troubles any one.'

"I could not discuss such extraordinary ideas. I diverted the conversation to the temperament of women. Chéron informed me that there were three kinds, those who were amorously disposed, those prompted by curiosity, and the third, indifferent. I thereupon asked her to which class she belonged.

"She looked at me somewhat haughtily and said:

" 'There are also various kinds of men. First and foremost are the impertinent ones . . .'

"Her reply caused her to appear far more contemporaneous than I had until then believed her to be. For that reason I began to speak to her the language used by me on similar occasions. After a few trifling and frivolous words I said to her:

" 'Will you grant me a favour and tell me your first name?'

" 'I have none!'

"She perceived that this seemed to vex me, for she resumed with some show of pique:

" 'Do you think that a woman must, in order to be pleasing to you, possess a first name, like the ladies of former days, a baptismal name, such as Marguerite, Thérèse, or Jeanne?'

" 'You are a living proof to the contrary.'

"I sought her gaze, but it did not respond to mine. She seemed not to have heard. I could no longer entertain doubts: she was a coquette. I was delighted. I told her that I found her charming, that I loved her, and I told her so over and over again. She suffered me to go on with my speeches, and finally asked:

" 'What do you mean by all this !'

"I became more pressing.

"She reproached me for taking liberties with her, exclaiming:

" 'Your ways are those of a savage.'

" 'I do not find acceptance with you?'

" 'I do not say so.'

" 'Chéron, Chéron, would it cost you any great effort to . . .'

"We sat down together on a bench over which an elm cast its shade. I took her hand, and carried it to my lips . . . of a sudden, I no longer felt, no longer saw anything, and I found myself lying in bed at home. I rubbed my eyes, smarting with the morning light, and I saw my valet who, standing before me with a stupid look, was saying to me:

" 'It is nine o'clock, sir. You told me to wake you at nine o'clock, sir. I have come to tell you, sir, that it is nine o'clock?' "

IPPOLYTE DUFRESNE was warmly congratulated by his friends on his finishing the reading of his story.

Nicole Langelier, applying to him the words of Critias to Triephon, said: "You seem to have dreamt on the white stone, in the midst of the people of dreams, since you dreamt so long a dream in the course of so short a night."

"It is not likely," remarked Joséphin Leclerc, "that the future will be such as you have seen it. I do not wish for the coming of socialism, but I dread it not. Collectivism at the helm would be quite another thing than is imagined. Who was it who said, carrying back his thoughts to the time of Constantine and of the Church's early triumphs: 'Christianity is triumphant, but its triumph is subject to the conditions imposed by life on all political and religious parties. All of them, whatever they may be, undergo so complete a transformation in the struggle that after victory there remains of themselves but the name and a few symbols of the last idea'?"

"Must we then give up the idea of knowing the future?" asked M. Goubin.

But Giacomo Boni, who when delving down into a few feet of soil had descended from the present period to the stone age, remarked:

"Upon the whole, humanity changes little. What has been shall be."

"No doubt," replied Jean Boilly, "man, or that which we call man, changes little. We belong to a definite species. The evolution of the species is of necessity included in the definition of the species. It is impossible to conceive humanity subsequent to its transformation. A transformed species is a lost species. But what reason is there for us to believe that man is the end of the evolution of life upon the earth? Why suppose that his birth has exhausted the creative forces of nature, and that the universal mother of the flora and fauna should, after having shaped him, become for ever barren. A natural philosopher, who does not stand in fear of his own ideas, H. G. Wells, has said: 'Man is not final.' No indeed, man is neither the beginning nor the end of terrestrial life. Long before him, all over the globe, animated forces were multiplying in the depths of the sea, in the mud of the strand, in the forests, lakes, prairies, and tree-topped mountains. After him, new forms will go on taking shape. A future race, born perhaps of our own, but having perchance no bond of origin with us, will succeed us in the empire of the planet. These new spirits of the earth will ignore or despise us. The monuments of our arts, should they discover vestiges of them, will have no meaning for them.   Rulers of the future, whose mind we can no more divine than the palæopithekos of the Siwalik Mountains was able to forecast the trains of thought of Aristotle, Newton, and Poincaré."

THE END

www.ingramcontent.com/pod-product-compliance
Lightning Source LLC
Chambersburg PA
CBHW050427260626
47156CB00003B/1184